The Goat Thief

The Goat Thief

Perumal Murugan

Translated by
N. Kalyan Raman

JUGGERNAUT BOOKS
C-I-128, First Floor, Sangam Vihar, Near Holi Chowk,
New Delhi 110080, India

First published in hardback by Juggernaut Books 2017
Published in paperback 2019

10 9 8 7 6 5 4 3 2

ISBN 978-93-5345-042-7

Typeset in Adobe Caslon Pro by R. Ajith Kumar, Noida

Printed and bound in India by Replika Press Pvt. Ltd.

For

Reji George Verghese

Contents

Preface

A World of Exceptions

In my experience, the short story is a highly challenging form in modern literature. Whenever I think of writing a short story, I am reminded of the art of drawing kolams practised in Tamil homes. The aim is to draw – during the early hours of morning, in the shadowy predawn light – a beautiful kolam at the entrance to your house. After spending a long time sweeping and cleaning the front yard, you pick up the kolam powder, and the idea that strikes you at that moment will take shape as the kolam. The simple one drawn with just four dots by a hand that weaves and crosses between them can be beautiful as never seen before. The grand one that is as wide as the street and drawn after hard practice over long hours can turn out to be an unsightly mess. Looking at the finished kolam from a distance, you may feel that something is amiss. A stray flower, picked up and placed at the centre, can erase the flaw and bring perfection to your doorway. It could be that nothing you do brings satisfaction and you move on, resigned to what seems fated for the day. It's the same with the short story.

Writing a new short story within the universe of the Tamil short story, which has thrived and flourished since the 1930s, can be challenging. More than any other form, it's in the short story that modern Tamil literature has brought off its greatest accomplishments. The number of short stories written in Tamil probably runs into hundreds of thousands; of them, at least several thousand pass muster. Among those, several hundred stand the test of time and endure. If a writer wants to write a short story that will take its place among those hundreds, an independent mind, a unique perspective on life and well-honed writing skills are essential.

When I started writing short stories, I didn't have any such awareness. As I wrote and read more and more over the years, I became conscious of these requirements. Taking them into consideration, I set aside the problem of form and started paying attention to the theme of the story. I realized all stories fall into one of two categories. The first category focuses on the problems of living according to the rules of society, while the second concentrates on exceptions to these rules. Both strategies have their advantages and disadvantages.

When he talks about rules, a writer can bring a story alive by striking a note of mild sorrow. And what is this sorrow? It is the wretchedness of taking every step in life with the fear that one might violate the rules. But it's never easy to focus on rules. It can be an uphill task to try to find a storyline inside that dreary world. On the other hand, exceptions can draw our attention easily. The lone goat that strays out of line inevitably appears distinct, doesn't it? At the same time, exceptions are subjected to derision, abuse and apathy, and constantly run the risk of being rejected.

It's my nature to feel concerned and affectionate towards those who are exceptions. They are afflicted with the misery of being unable to live according to rules. They face endless harassment and vilification. Isolating themselves from others, they create their own private worlds. Nevertheless, they experience the immense joy that transgression brings. They are the ones who render the old rules defunct and lead us to new ways of being. They function to the best of their creative abilities. In this way, they fulfil their historical role of taking society forward. My own choice is to know and to follow the rules, and to live under their authority. Even so, I look upon this as a stepping stone to a mode of conscious defiance.

Talking about exceptions requires great courage. One false step, and the rules will turn up in their thousands like a giant swarm of ants and tear your flesh apart. I've written with a sense of caution; I've written without it too. What can I do? Exceptions have the seductive power to make you forget yourself. Once we are trapped by the magic of their allure, we can no longer carve our own path. They will take us wherever they want. Everything we encounter along the way is bound to be new: new sights, new beings, new objects. Exceptions have a way of demanding and bestowing new perspectives.

Preface

Ten years ago, I published a collection of stories called *Pee Kadaigal* (Shit Tales). I know people who were furious on hearing the title, others who were ashamed to buy the book, still others who felt too shy to carry it in their hands after having bought it, those who took it home and kept it under wraps, and those who read it in secret. For all that, the stories in the collection were just plain, ordinary tales. All that the tales did was expose what were classified as euphemisms in traditional Tamil grammar and were hidden out of sight. Even today, when I am introduced at a literary meeting, *Pee Kadaigal* is not included in the list of books authored by me. I've always considered the omission inadvertent and habitually referred to it in my subsequent talk. For, why would a person who writes of 'The World of Exceptions' worry overmuch about civility and refinement?

I wrote my first short story in 1988, and I have written more than eighty short stories so far. This book is a selection of ten stories, and the only criterion for their selection is the successful realization of the form. All these stories are about exceptions. Therefore, I place them, radiant as they are with the seductive allure and fresh perspectives characteristic of exceptions, before the reader.

I wish to thank the translator N. Kalyan Raman, who has wonderfully assimilated these stories, enhanced my dialect-inflected prose style and translated them into English; Juggernaut Books for publishing the first collection of my stories in English translation; and my friend Kalachuvadu Kannan who undertook all the efforts required to make this book possible.

3 September 2017
Namakkal, Tamil Nadu

Perumal Murugan

1

The Well

He seemed reluctant when they invited him. 'Me?' he mumbled softly, as if to himself. But in his gleaming heart, newly cleansed of moss-like memories, desire and eagerness swelled and rose. The children began to badger him further. He had come there as a guest. He was in fact a fairly close relative. Because he hadn't visited them often, he couldn't be totally at ease. A short while later, the children – three of them between the ages of eight and twelve: two boys and a girl – were ready to roll around on his lap and use him as a referee for their games. This invitation had come as the high point of that readiness. He was excited, feeling a mild thrill in his heart, as if he had just received a long-submerged memento. He couldn't get up immediately and leave with them. The fine threads of diffidence had bound his feet. His perspiring soles had turned the floor beneath them damp and sticky. He filled his eyes with desire and let them wander about aimlessly. His voice choked in his throat. Crinkling their eyes, the children touched his jaw and pleaded with him, grabbed his hand possessively and pulled him up. As he got up with a jerk, the cot screeched and made a loud noise. He was afraid that some voice might command them, 'Don't disturb him, da' and disrupt the situation. He thought it would be wise to leave with them before that happened. He restrained his eagerness and said in a tone of offering a concession, 'But I haven't brought a towel,' like it was a major problem. Shouting excitedly, the children rushed everywhere and brought a towel each. With a shy smile spreading over his features, he got up from the cot.

Amid the fields pervaded by the smell of vegetation, the well appeared suddenly like the gaping mouth of the land. The well had neither proper walls nor a regular shape. It looked open and desolate, with flab bulging out in places and wounds in the form of pit holes all over. There was a foot-worn track going down that resembled a series of steps. The pipe from the motor was half submerged in the water and quite still. Sunlight that passed through coconut fronds penetrated the water to reveal the sand at the bottom. It was a well whose very appearance would make anyone's legs itch to jump in. The children were arguing and fighting over which of them should jump in first. Only the beginning was important. It was enough to hear the splash, followed by the sloshing of water. The frozen silence of the well had to be broken first. After that, the frenzy would infect everyone. The difficulty was in getting started, unhampered by dread that the well was waiting to claim the first one who jumped as votive sacrifice. Undressed by now, the children continued their bickering. Even as the children's attention was focused on fighting among themselves, he dived neatly into the well, like a ripe coconut detaching itself from a bunch and dropping to the ground. Immediately the children jumped in, one by one, from each corner of the well. Now the once-frozen well began to speak through a variety of sounds. There was the constant noise of water splashing and colliding against the walls. The children had trails they could clamber up to jump into the well again. As if their sole aim that day was to torment the water by jumping in, the splash and sloshing that followed jumping were heard continuously.

He experienced the well differently. While swimming, he stroked the water gently, as if he was embracing a flower-soft baby. The irregular shape of the well gave him immense pleasure. As the sun was really hot, the coldness of the water felt like a poultice all over the body. He enjoyed dunking his head frequently under water; he also liked swimming on his back. The sun's rays which had scattered on the well came looking for him as he lay inside that deep hollow and struck him on the face. The well held a hoard of miracles within, and was giving it to him, little by little. Intense ardour for the well bloomed in his heart. He craved to caress and embrace its every speck. He spent a long time travelling towards each of its corners which were strewn with cobwebs pushed aside by the sloshing water. Each corner formed a small niche where a person could stand and rest – or at least had formations like railings that a swimmer could hold on to. The well was full of compassion. In the corners, he experienced the pleasure of ice-cold water. He wanted to plunge towards the depths and get to know the well's nether parts. A few seconds after going down the centre of the well, he sensed that he had submerged a long way inside. The well stretched even deeper. Unable to grasp how deep and how long he had travelled, he struggled to breathe. He pressed his hands down quickly and rose upward. There were so many secrets inside the well. Was it going to unpack and spread them out in barely a few minutes for an occasional visitor like him? What kind of fool am I, he scolded himself. He sat on a flat stone slab near the steps leading upward and relaxed a little. He eyed with fresh wonder the frogs that clung to the walls with every shift of the water as well as those that leapt into the water from above. He felt for a brief while that he was merely a spectator at the well.

The children did not tire at all. Ignoring the mud sliding down from the walls, they kept climbing up and jumping off by turns. He saw little difference between them and the frogs. He felt that the well was watching them with gentle amusement that was like a smile rising to an old man's lips. When the girl stretched and jumped, with her tassel loose and ribbon fluttering in the wind, it was as if the well obediently received and held up a little angel as she descended amid the splendour of sunshine. The boys were so quick that their climbing up or jumping down went by in a blur. The well proudly accepted their meaningless shouts. It was perhaps relishing all these capers with the attitude of someone who had been engrossed in companionless solitude for too long and was tired of it. The secret breeze that embraced his body caused a chill. All the droplets that rolled down from his body had mingled with the well. Once the body was dry, the tremors began. The cold he didn't feel while he was in the water gripped him suddenly when he went up a little. In fact, it was the well's trickery. Its invitation to step in. If a man visited once, the well cast a spell that goaded him to return again and again. He dived through a wave. Now lukewarm water caressed his skin and embraced him. Without being conscious of it, he thought of the well as a circle and swam a full round. Though the traces of his leg strokes kept disappearing instantly, the eddies remained. They induced him to swim another round. Meanwhile, the little girl called out to him:

'Chittappa, how many rounds can you go without stopping?'

He was unable to give her a number. He scanned the well. Its expanse, devoid of sharp angles, did not lead him to any conclusion. Not having an answer, he offered a bland, evasive smile. She was adamant.

'Can you do ten rounds?'

The boy answered her question: 'Chittappa can't even swim two.'

Though he could sense that the boy had said it only to provoke him, he was of a mind to give it a try and face the challenge. A round consisted of starting from the step, touching every corner, one by one, and returning to the step. By the time he finished the first round and was midway through the second, his respiratory organs felt weak from the strain. He started breathing through the mouth. His arms were tired and his legs refused to cooperate. However much he tried, he simply could not go on. The well had defeated him again. Stopping at a corner, he doubled over and gasped for breath. Their shouts were so loud and deafening that he wondered if the well itself was rejoicing in his defeat. The shouts compounded his humiliation. He wanted to climb up and go away. The well was a universe that no one could conquer.

He had to accept his defeat. To compete with it and lose was in itself an act of courage. He sighed with a swell of pride. He swam towards the step. His arms stroked the water with the pious modesty of a devotee holding the rope of a sacred chariot. On reaching the steps, he took a last dip, combed his hair back with the water and said:

'I'm going up. If you want to keep playing, come back after you're done.'

His announcement must have given them a rude shock. For a few moments, there was no sound except the gentle sloshing of water in the well. A pall of sorrow had settled on the little girl's face. The boys looked dejected. They couldn't accept that the pleasures of the well had to end so soon. If he got out of the well, they had to follow suit. They were not permitted to be in the well without any adult to mind them. The well harboured so many threats within. There could be venomous old snakes hatching in the holes high above the water. In some evil moment, those snakes might stretch their heads and come out. There could be hidden rock cavities that trapped and dragged underwater swimmers inside. There was the ever-present danger of slipping and plummeting under water. Adults could handle such situations, but children...? Moreover, it was a lone well sloshing at the centre of a ring of tall coconut trees. It looked haunted. The echo of voices could arrive from any direction. An eerie silence had come to dwell permanently in the black water. If the man who was a protective shield against all these dangers went up, it was the end. The little girl started again in the same pleading tone that she had used to invite him to the well.

'No, chittappa. Some more time, chittappa.'

Her pleas did not affect him now in any way. He was resolute in his decision to leave. With a disdainful smile on his face, he took another step forward. From where she was standing in the east corner, the girl leapt effortlessly in the water and came near him. She clung tightly to his legs. Drenched hair swaying, she begged him, 'Don't go, chittappa.' He had not expected this. Her hands held his legs like a snake twisted and wound around them. 'Let go, kannu...let go,' he said. He imagined that these ordinary words were enough to free him of her obstinacy. But she would not let him go. I won't let go till you grant me a boon, her bent figure seemed to plead with him.

He didn't understand any of it. In his confusion, he bent down and tried gently to prise her fingers from his legs. Her grip only grew tighter instead of loosening.

'Don't let him get away, girl,' a voice called out from somewhere. Even then he thought it was the playful stubbornness of children and responded with a relaxed laugh. At an unexpected moment, the girl's hands swept his legs off the step and pushed him inside. As a stone protruding from a wall comes loose and drops, he fell into the water with a loud splash. The water-whip struck him a hard blow on the stomach. Electrons of fear raced through his entire body. He gathered himself and swam back to the step. He wondered if this too was a defeat at the hands of the well. Pretending that it was nothing like that, he spoke to the girl in an appeasing tone – 'Why did you do that, kannu?' – as he started climbing up. Now the older boy was standing on the step – not really a step, just a stone protruding from the wall – above him. The boy spread his arms wide and swung them up and down while he shouted, 'I'm not going to let you pass!' As he lifted a leg, determined to make his way up, the boy bent down, hugged his neck and rolled over. Both fell together into the well. He dragged the boy into the water and, thrusting his leg forward, gave him a hard push downward before swimming back quickly to the step. The boy could return only after touching the mud at the bottom. He pushed hard at the girl who came at him aiming to clasp his neck, and leapt on to the steps. 'Ei!' With an energetic bellow, another boy jumped on him. It was an entirely unexpected moment. He dropped into the water again. His eyes were dazzled by the light that came boring through the water. He tried to see through the droplets. There were only incomprehensible sights everywhere. He grew agitated. There was no way to escape other than climbing up and running for it. But there was another boy just above the step. Suddenly, a kind of order had come about among them: one to struggle with him in the water, one to clutch his legs and prevent him from climbing on to the step, and one standing above to jump on him and bring him down. They occupied their respective positions by turns. They had morphed into a heavy shackle around him that couldn't be broken.

For how long could he continue playing this

game? What was this game, anyway? It was only the well's cunning trick disguised as a game. He had not visited anyone's house as a guest. The well had brought him. No one had invited him to swim. The well had sent its emissaries in human form. He didn't know their faces. The well was the fount of all illusion. It was a death pit, asking for votive sacrifice. He had conveniently got trapped inside the well's gigantic maw. How wrong he was to think they were children. Three demons who were foot servants of the well. One leapt at him, aiming for his neck. One pulled him off his feet. One rolled around and wrestled with him under water. Their laughs were invitations that would suck the life out of him. The little demons were crazed with hunger. How could he ever get away?

The pit holes on the walls of the well turned into dark caves where death was hiding itself. The water was an acid solution that burnt the skin black. Did he possess enough strength as a swimmer to triumph over these? Climbing on to the walls, the toads stood there with their spinning eyes and gaping mouths. They were ready to knock him down at any moment. When the demons wilted from exhaustion, the toads could pounce on him. Fear spread through his entire body and dropped anchor there. It didn't even permit him to think about anything. Driven more and more by the urge to go up and escape, he tried again and again, sliding back into the well each time. His belly was bloated from swallowing all that water. Tremors had taken root in his entire body. All the scrapes and wounds in many parts of his body from those awkward falls were now inflamed. He ignored all of it. He remained focused on escaping. Their aim was to destroy him little by little and finally devour him, it seemed. He turned fierce like a terrified animal battling certain death. He caught and thrashed the demons that came to capture him. He pushed them with a thrust of his leg towards the bottom of the well. But their fury, too, grew to match his.

This death pit might have some other exit paths. He leapt towards a corner. He could hardly stand. His legs were shaking. Sweat flowed more profusely than the water streaming down his body. Taking his move to the corner as their victory, those demons jumped for joy. His searching eyes fell on the motor pipe. His hands flew with the urgency of finding a hold. Clutching the pipe, he started climbing swiftly. He guessed that it was the only way available to get out from there. As he climbed, he had to battle very hard with the pipe's smooth body. Although it shook this way and that, it held strong, without changing position. The climactic frenzy of the game had caught everywhere. These might be the very moments that decided victory and defeat. As he kept climbing, a figure resembling a large blob of treacle came sliding down the pipe at great speed and dashed against him. His grip slackened and he fell straight into the water. That was it. Everything was decided, it seemed to him. He began to babble incoherently. His arms were involuntarily stroking the water. He didn't know in which direction he was swimming. He couldn't sense where the hold was. His hands clutched at all manner of things. His trembling legs climbed on to something else. It might have been a parapet of the well. His hands seemed to be grasping the edges of protruding stones. He felt that he had climbed some distance. It gave him confidence and drew him up. He vaulted further and further. Then the well raised its voice and echoed: 'Snake! Snake!' His hands went limp and his grip came loose. With his mouth agape and limbs splayed wide, he fell on his back into the water, like a frog.

Translated from 'Neer Vilaiyattu'

2

The Wailing of a Toilet Bowl

The sour smell started from the kitchen and spread throughout the apartment. The door, which was always shut and secured by a chain, and the windowless walls would not allow it to escape. When the man – or, occasionally, the woman – undid the chain and opened the door, the smell curled into a ball and raced towards the entrance. Meanwhile, the door would have turned back into a wall, tightly shut again.

The smell did not affect her in any way; she wanted their apartment to be permeated with it at all times. Inhaling the smell pleased her heart and streamlined its functioning. Whenever her husband was relaxed enough to notice the smell, he wrinkled his nose a little, that was all. He knew that it was a foul smell. It had been many years since he had come to accept such things as normal. He had neither the interest nor the time to investigate the source. Sexual intercourse, a recent addition to his daily routine, ensured that he got up late in the morning. He woke up with a start, as if by the flick of a switch. Once he was up, his only aim was to get ready fast and leave for office. Why would he care about anything else?

From the time her husband left for work until his return at dusk, she thought obsessively about the smell. Her problem was not the smell, which rose from the soggy rice fermenting in the large aluminium vat of leftover food in the kitchen, but the capacity of the vat. Somehow half a bowl of cooked rice soaked in water ended up in the vat every day. She knew that she should reduce the quantity of rice, but she couldn't help dropping an extra fistful into the cooker. As she held the raw rice in her hand, her mind would insist that she throw it back into the rice bag. But she couldn't stop asking herself: 'What if somebody called on us suddenly?' The hesitant hand won in the end. The extra rice inevitably ended up in the vat. Regardless of the number of times she mashed the soaked rice and drank it during the day, the quantity of stale rice in the vat remained the same.

Her husband wouldn't touch it, and she didn't want to serve it to him either.

In the one week since her arrival, no guest had come to their fourth-floor apartment in the multistoreyed building. Though the city was teeming with her husband's friends and relatives, none had visited them. She was perplexed. She didn't understand how people could meet up in places other than their homes. When she asked him, he snapped at her: 'So who should I bring along, then?' She had married her maternal uncle, a mid-level official in the government, and moved from her village in the remote interior to this bustling metropolis. Her arrival had given him a couple of nipples to bite into and a hole to copulate in; that was enough for him. Though she was aroused by his hairy chest and blunt-tipped penis, she couldn't spend all her waking hours thinking about him. To pass the time, she planned to turn her attention to other activities. She wanted to sweep the floor in front of the door, sprinkle water and draw a kolam as big as a garden patch every day. She had filled a few notebooks with the kolam patterns she had practised before marriage. But the sticker kolam that was pasted at the entrance to her apartment, an area so small that it could be covered by just four or five pairs of slippers, was permanent. She had pleasant fantasies about how little girls from neighbouring apartments would come looking for her, fondly call her akka, and get her to braid their hair; and how she would tell them stories while she tried out new braiding patterns on them every day. But she couldn't even find out when exactly the shut doors of her neighbours opened and the girls went out. Could it be that no little girls lived in their building?

Her only companions in the daytime were the slivers of sunlight in the kitchen, which entered through the ventilator high on the wall. They didn't worry at all about the foul smell. They landed on the opposite wall at a particular hour and, just like her husband, moved away imperceptibly while pretending to stay on, and vanished all of a sudden. Had her husband put them in their apartment as a substitute for his presence? Once they too had left, she felt weary and dejected. If she spoke to her husband about how time weighed heavily on her, he pointed to her lower abdomen and said with a leer, 'It'll be all right once you get something in there.' Overcome by shyness, she was unable to say anything more.

With no way to escape, the sour smell pressed against the walls and flowed downward. She never imagined that she would let it come this far. When she poured the leftover rice into the vat the previous day, she had planned to catch the milkman in the morning and offer it to him. His cow would happily chew and gobble up the rice. She couldn't find out at what time the milkman dropped the milk packet in the empty plastic bag that was hung on the metal gate outside the main door. Regardless of the hour at which she woke up – six, five or four – when she opened the door and checked, the packet would be there. It was a miracle beyond her comprehension. Spotting the milkman became a challenge. She tried sleeping next to the front door so she could get up as soon as she heard any sound. But before she could open the door, the sound of the milkman's footsteps would have reached the floor above. She couldn't even manage to glimpse his shirt tail.

If she asked one of her neighbours, she might hit upon a solution, she thought. She could also be on speaking terms with them. She stood outside the entrance to her flat for a long time, waiting for someone to pass by. That doors were meant to remain shut was apparently the rule prescribed and followed here. Bracing herself, she went over diffidently to the doorway of the adjacent flat and rang the bell. After making her quiver in anxiety for a few minutes, a voice called out from behind the half-open door: 'Who is it?' When she introduced herself as the neighbour from the adjacent flat, a fair-skinned woman came out, flashed a thin smile and said, 'What do you want?' After explaining to her about the sour smell, she enquired if any cattle owner came to the building. The woman must have felt like making fun of her; however, displaying only an amused smile, she said with finality, 'I don't know. We never have any leftover rice in our house.' Before she could think up other lines of enquiry – don't you have any guests coming to your house, hasn't there been at least one day when you cooked excess rice, where do you pour the water drained from the cooked rice – the woman had shut the door and retreated inside.

The vat was filling up fast. It would overflow in the next couple of days. Before that happened, she had to find some way to empty it. After her husband left for the office, she locked their apartment and went down to the ground floor. She was confident that somewhere down the road she could find the house of a milkman who reared cows and buffaloes. As far as the eye could see, there were only multistoreyed apartment buildings on both sides. She was scared to move from there. Even if she walked a short distance away, she would find it impossible to recognize her building and reach home. All the buildings were of the same height and painted a uniform colour, without any variation. She was amazed that her husband identified their apartment correctly and reached home every day. What if he made a mistake one day and went to the wrong apartment? Just thinking about it made her feel agitated. But he was a smart man, who was aware of subtle distinctions. Just as he had done all these days, he would continue to come straight home without losing his way. Telling herself such things over and over again, she suppressed her sense of panic. She did not see any cattle or milkman. After waiting there for a long time, she climbed up the stairs to their flat.

Like the foam in a mug of toddy, the rice in the vat foamed and swelled, giving off a smell that struck her as soon as she opened the door. On seeing the foam bubbles burst, she thought that the soaked rice must be weeping. When she realized that she had entered a world in which she couldn't even talk about such things to anyone, she became frightened. She had heard that people were densely packed in a city, and seen it in films as well. She wondered whether her husband had lied to her that they were living in a city, and had instead settled her in the desolate interior of a forest. It wasn't yet time for him to come home. The sliver of sunlight was now crawling across the kitchen wall. Lying on the floor with her head near the door, she dozed off. When the calling bell exploded inside her head, she got up hurriedly and opened the door. Though he had warned her many times that she should look through the peephole in the door and ascertain who it was before opening the door, she didn't remember it in her haste. After scolding her for the lapse, he walked in with a weary expression on his face.

She didn't even have the patience to wait till he had taken off his shirt. Disheartened by her defeated attempts, she burst into tears. Her husband was annoyed at being received by a sleepy and tear-stained face. 'What is it?' That single question was enough to assuage her feelings. When she told him, through a combination of sobs and words, all about the sour smell and her failure to get rid of it, compassion flowed like a wellspring in his heart. Guilt about having paid no attention to her problems brought a look of tenderness to his face. Still wearing his unbuttoned shirt, he went straight to the kitchen and lifted the vat. The thin solution of soaked rice sloshed around like buttermilk in a churning pot. He opened the door that led to the bathroom and the toilet situated right next to the kitchen and carried the vat inside. She was not sure what he was going to do next. He turned the vat upside down over the toilet bowl. The rice was deposited in shit. After swallowing all the rice from a large vat in barely a second, the toilet bowl shrilled a great trumpeting cry and waited with its mouth wide open for more. Leering at her suggestively, it threw her a crooked grin. Her face turned white in terror as she flung her arms around her husband.

Keeping both palms open, the toilet bowl had

assumed the shape of a skull. The fear that swelled in her heart wouldn't allow her to even look at the beast. She didn't have the strength to go anywhere near the toilet. She made sure that its door was always shut but continued to worry that despite her precaution the door might swing open at a moment when she was completely immersed in cooking. After placing something on the stove, she would turn with a start towards the door. The toilet bowl shook and rattled the door from the inside. At any minute, the door might open and the toilet bowl might step out with its copra shell mouth wide open. She would draw the outside bolt fully shut and return to her cooking. She was confident that nothing untoward would happen when her husband was at home. At a mere wave of his hand, the toilet bowl would retreat with its tail between its legs and embed itself once again on the bathroom floor, she guessed. But after he left home, the toilet bowl would scream and howl with its ever-increasing hunger pangs. She did not move. She bolted the kitchen door as well and came out. To drown out the screams, she turned up the radio and sat down in the hall.

If the toilet bowl was not satisfied with

swallowing a whole vat of rice, and asked for more with its mouth open and a wheedling grin, how could anyone feed its hunger? The solution of leftover rice was accumulating in the vat again and she could ask her husband to pour it in the toilet bowl after a few days. But what was it seeking with its open mouth? It was bent on devouring her, she thought. She had to stay beyond the reach of its ugly din and yowls of hunger. As soon as she stepped into the kitchen, her whole body was assaulted by its silent scream. Her only prayer was that its ear-splitting cry should not travel beyond the kitchen. Her husband remained deaf to its screams. He was like an inert object crawling around the apartment. With an insatiably hungry beast in the house, how was he able to walk about as he pleased, ignoring its horrible screams? Was it because he was strong enough to tame it? She was disfigured by the daily torment of trying to escape its clutches during the day. She became skin and bone. The sheen of a new bride was ruined and her breasts wilted. All the freshness of a fertile, young woman left her. She feared that her skull might turn white and she might come to resemble the toilet bowl.

Feeling disappointed after caressing her wrinkled, lifeless breasts repeatedly in the night, her husband was moved to ask her if something was wrong. Once the tears had gushed forth from her and drowned the bed, she told him haltingly about the toilet bowl. He laughed and gathered her into the crook of his arm. She realized on that day that the affection behind the embrace had always been latent in him. She was even more shocked by his words.

'There's a scent coming off your body, the smell of a juicy ear of pearl millet combined with that of a tender stalk. It seems like the toilet bowl can't stand that particular smell.'

All the splendours of her body returned and became a part of her in that very instant. That he had known so accurately the scent of her body was enough for her. She learnt that he still kept the dust-coated records of childhood safe from damage in the attics of his mind.

He said, 'If this odour leaves you, the beast will become docile, like it is with me.'

At that moment, her mind was occupied more by him than the toilet. Her face fell when she heard his words.

'Does it mean you don't like how I smell?'

As the strain of the previous days melted away, he smiled. 'I like it very much, but you have to change it to something the beast will like.'

From the next day on, suppressing the panic that gripped her the moment she heard its voice, she pacified the toilet bowl from a distance, talking indulgently as if to a pet: 'Just wait for a few more days, won't you please?' Using an expensive bathing soap gifted by her husband, rubbing it copiously on her body and luxuriating under a blanket of lather, she bathed for a long time in a corner of the kitchen. Applying an assortment of fresh creams on her face and body and lounging in front of the mirror became her main task during the day. The entire apartment became fragrant with the scent of soap and the pleasant odour of various creams. The wails of the toilet bowl seemed to have subsided a little. Even so, she couldn't bring herself to step boldly into the bathroom when her husband was not at home. The open mouth and obscene grin were still there to greet her. A streak of mischief flashed at the corner of the toilet bowl's puckered mouth. She could not control the generosity of her hand either. Gone were the days when she expected a guest to arrive at any time. Now her hand put an extra measure of rice into the cooker only to quench the howling appetite of the toilet bowl. So the sequence of events continued as before: the vat filled up fast with the solution of stale rice; her husband lifted it up and poured its entire contents into the toilet bowl; after fleeing to the bedroom and bolting the door, she would cover herself fully with a blanket before lying down to sleep.

Every night, as she lay in his arms, she asked her husband, 'Did you smell the ear of pearl millet today?' He sniffed her again and again to the point of dizziness and whispered, 'Yes.' She was stricken with sorrow at her inability to change her smell in spite of trying everything she could think of. 'It doesn't come from your body,' he mumbled. She was growing more and more disheartened by the day. The wails, which had dwindled to low whimpers and mumbles, became louder and more frequent again. As her hitherto suppressed fear rose to the surface, she realized that the toilet bowl was prepared to gobble her up any moment. She wrote home to her parents and in-laws. They didn't know anything about toilet bowls. The replies she received were predictable:

'Do as your husband tells you.'

Apart from the comforting words he babbled in her ear during intimate moments, she got little else from her husband. On top of everything, when she heard the toilet bowl groaning, she felt extremely annoyed and angry. Stringing together all the profane invectives she knew, she flung abuse at her adversary continuously. In response, the toilet bowl started howling louder than ever before. She realized that as its hunger grew more and more acute, and became intolerable, the toilet bowl was calling out to her like an entitled intimate. Still trapped by the agony of having to pour rice into shit, she closed her eyes, carried the vat to the latrine herself and emptied it into the toilet bowl. She would be sweating profusely by the time she finished and came back. If she ever opened her eyes slightly and looked around, she would be done for. 'You're the one I want. I want you,' the toilet bowl would bare its teeth in a grin and pounce on her. It would try to raise its outstretched arms towards her. Scared out of her wits, she would run away from there, panting. To forestall such a situation, she took several precautionary measures. She finished her morning ablutions in a hurry while her husband was still at home. She came out of the kitchen immediately after his departure and opened it again only after his return. She paid no heed to the constant howling from inside the bathroom.

In spite of all her precautions, the dreaded event did come to pass one day. When she entered the bathroom around dawn, casually stretching her arms above her head to cast off the laziness, she had, as usual, not bolted the door. She also kept her eyes closed. After she was done, when she tried to step out, she must have placed her foot awkwardly on the rim of the toilet bowl. In the blink of an eye, the smooth cavity snared her foot and pulled her inside. Recovering her wits, she held on to the top edge with both hands. The toilet bowl, which had swallowed her up to the neck, tried to grunt and draw her in completely. She held fast to the rim and kept calling out to her husband. The toilet bowl choked her. She yelled despite the deathly grip around her throat. Still

only half-awake, her husband mumbled to himself
inside an early morning dream, rolled over happily
and went back to sleep.

Translated from 'Pee Vaangiyin Olam'

3

Musical Chairs

When they came to live in the house, they found a chair – drowned in dust and host to a gang of spiders residing in cobwebs – abandoned like an orphan in a corner. Though not an antique, the chair looked so elegant that it seemed to demand placement in a house.

Once the chair was wiped clean and placed in the hall, its beauty bestowed a lustre to that spacious house. Traces of past use were present as scratch marks all over its body. Some of those might have even been scars. But the chair wasn't really disfigured by those marks.

After all the items had been arranged in suitable spots around the house, the presence of the chair, with its rich legacy of experience, gave them the feeling that there was one more person living with them. They took turns sitting on it, and enjoyed themselves. Nearly always, their conversation revolved around the chair.

When they saw the big veranda in front of the house, both of them had imagined how grand the space would look with a chair in it. That it became reality was indeed a gift of providence. With a pleasure akin to holding her in his arms, he lifted the chair, carried it outside and kept it on the veranda. She blushed on seeing the ardent expression on his face. While he sat with his feet resting on the parapet wall, she brought him a cup of hot tea.

He got up immediately and perched on the parapet, yielding the chair to her. It was a joyful moment for her. She wished with all her heart that her entire life would pass in the same loving ambience. He smiled proudly at her.

He experienced the special pleasure of sipping the tea while gazing at her cheerful face. That their landlord had built such a wonderful house didn't seem a feat to them. They praised him for leaving behind a treasure like that chair to adorn the house. They considered the chair a pet that belonged to both of them. When he was out of the house during the day, she was comforted by its presence as a steadfast companion.

When he returned in the evenings, the chair gave him a lap to sit on and rest. He put his feet up on a shelf of the wall cupboard and listened to the radio or read books. Sometimes he even curled up in the chair and went to sleep. It supported him, standing on its bent legs. He slept peacefully, free of disturbance. She liked to gaze at him tenderly while he slept.

Friends dropped in all the time to see him. As soon as a friend arrived, he would offer the chair to the visitor and sit leaning against the wall. If they were on the veranda outside, he would sit on the parapet wall. Many of his friends seemed to visit him only for the opportunity to sit on that chair. She would be busy in the kitchen, either preparing refreshments for the visitors or doing other chores. The chair was in demand whenever he was at home.

He never budged from the chair. If she was sitting on it when he was around, he felt irritated. 'I've come back after wandering all over. Can't I sit down for a while if I want to?' Often, she would wearily get up the moment he started complaining. It was implied that she could well have sat on the chair for most of the day when it lay empty. She was afraid that he might even forget her in his obsession with the chair. Over time, she grew upset at the very sight of the chair and often grumbled.

'We need to buy another chair.'

He pretended not to have heard her. Sometimes he'd nod his head lightly and say, 'Hmm,' as if only to himself. She grumbled more and more. Soon she had nothing to communicate to him except complaints. The grumbling that welcomed him when he entered the house didn't let up until he stepped out again. At the moment of his departure, it all rose as one voice and drove him out.

He would hurry away with his head bowed. When it was clear that he couldn't handle it any more, he laid out the monthly budget before her. In that list, income was well short of expenditure. Just as he had anticipated, it stopped her grumbling for a few days, but there was no lasting benefit. Since she was past the stage of being able to force herself to stop, it came out without her being conscious of it. He started giving her lectures.

He lectured her without hesitation at all hours.

His homilies revolved around the difficulties of running a household in a big city, the cost of living which kept climbing every day and their sorry situation where he couldn't even buy the clothes he needed.

He strictly refrained from talking about the chair. She knew that the chair was the true subject of his lectures. Whenever she was angry, he would sense it, tactfully get off the chair and sit on the floor. He would also observe from the corner of his eye whether she made a move to sit on it.

She hated the very idea of sitting on that chair. She wouldn't go anywhere near it even when he was not at home. She had begun to think that it belonged exclusively to him. Sitting on it in his absence felt like a sneaky thing to do. Asking for a share in what had become his was demeaning to her. She indicated to him in a whole lot of ways that she could live in peace only if she had a chair of her own. Ignoring his harangues, she scooped them up along with the garbage and flung them outside. On one occasion, when he raised his foul-smelling voice at her, she gnashed her teeth and screamed at him:

'This is *your* wretched possession, not mine.'

He calmed down after that. He also stopped declaiming that she was free to sit on the chair. Nevertheless, he wasn't at all keen on buying a new chair or submitting to her whims.

When he handed the monthly accounts to her as usual, she threw a big tantrum, tore it up and threw the pieces away. Though he understood that he *had* to buy her a new chair that month, he stomped off as though he was very angry. But nothing happened as she had feared and desired: he returned home soon. There was a brand-new chair in his hands.

As if tossing aside an unwanted object, he dumped the chair carelessly in a corner, and then removed his shirt. When she saw the chair, she no longer cared a whit about him or the expression on his face. As if hugging a child, she extended both arms and lifted the chair. Though this chair was not as attractive as that old one, its varnished glitter made her proud. Her bright face and the gleaming chair spread cheer and happiness throughout the house.

This chair could be unfolded and folded as necessary. It could be put away when not in use. There was no need to worry that someone might sit on it. She looked at the old chair with ridicule in her eyes and gave a disdainful smile. Her husband was slumped wearily on it. Just as it had been on their first day in that house, a sense of calm pervaded the entire house.

She didn't even like the smell of the old chair. She never went anywhere near it, nor did she talk about it. She was glued to her chair. Like him, she also slept in the chair. As if to wreak vengeance on him, she even lived in it. He and his chair had become adversaries she didn't have to bother about. She lounged in the outer veranda just as he did. She lifted her feet and rested them on the parapet wall. She leaned back in her chair and read books, listened to the radio. Placing a small cardboard pad across the two armrests, she pretended to write random notes; sometimes, she actually wrote too.

Now and again, she felt a rush of pity for him. That he eventually bought her the chair, even if he had wantonly delayed it for a while, filled her with compassion. Sometimes she brooded about having treated him so cruelly in her quest for a chair. That he never tried to lay any claim to her chair made her feel even more affectionate. How did he find out that she had mellowed? She didn't know.

That evening, while he was talking to a friend who had dropped in to see him, she went inside to make tea. He got up from his perch on the wall and very rightfully sat down on her chair. Though he was sitting on it for the very first time he felt very cosy, and experienced no discomfort. He said something casually to his friend and laughed. When she came back with the tea, she offered him a gentle smile of acceptance. She might have thought that this was her chance to make amends for the cruelties she had inflicted on him for so long.

Her smile gave him courage. After it became clear that he didn't need to be nervous about her behaviour, he'd turn slightly in her direction whenever there was a visitor. As if she understood, she too would get up with a smile and go inside.

He or his friend would sit down on her chair. She would sit leaning against a wall inside the house and busy herself with some chore. When most evenings came to be spent in this fashion, panic engulfed her. Might he grab the new chair too? Would this chair too slip out of her hands like the old one? Though she consoled herself in various ways – that this happened only when friends dropped in, that he wasn't such a bad person – she was still upset.

Every evening, she took the chair inside the house and sat down on it. Let him sit on the wall like before. She told him that the evening breeze did not suit her health. He too nodded his head as if in agreement. Even so, whenever there was a visitor, he would turn towards the hall and call out to her. As soon as she entered the kitchen to make tea, he would follow her in and take her chair away. She always folded the chair and left it leaning on the wall. This made it easier for him to take it away.

Inside the house too, whenever she wasn't sitting on it, he would unfold her chair, put his feet up on it and read or listen to the radio. On one such evening, she lunged angrily and drew her chair back. Her fiery breath conveyed her outrage: why did he keep his feet on that chair, like he was insulting her?

Since she had pulled the chair back at an unexpected moment, his feet hit the ground suddenly and he stumbled a little. He was surprised that she was still staking a claim on that chair. Only then was he reminded of the fact that she never sat on his chair, not even by mistake.

From that day, he behaved like a man who had learnt how to show respect and refrained from using the chair to rest his feet. But he would use it now and again as a table for keeping books or teacups.

As the days passed, she was afraid that he might say it was not really a chair, plunk sundry objects on it and push it close to the wall. When she thought about how she had ended up with a blockhead who couldn't even treat a chair as a chair, it felt as if her heart might explode. 'Learn that this is a chair first,' she was getting ready to scream aloud at any moment.

Meanwhile, there came along a government-sponsored general strike. Since the government had declared the strike with the noble intention of letting tired workers relax for a day, there was no chance that even a small shop would be open. There were programmes on the radio all day long. The expectation that he was going to stay home during the daytime as well made her very happy. She wanted to cook something special for him.

They slept till long after sunup. She finished her morning chores at a leisurely pace and cooked him a simple breakfast. A friend dropped in around midday. Though it wasn't as if they were meeting after a long time, there was such joy in their conversation. They decided to celebrate that special day.

But neither was keen on going out; and there was no use going out, anyway. After all, didn't they wander about in the outside world every single day? A pack of cards proved a handy solution to their predicament. They improvised a card table by keeping two large vessels upside down on the floor and a rough wooden plank across. They sat facing each other on the two chairs. They were aware of the world only up to that point. Then, through the kings and queens of the card pack, their world was made anew. Apart from the occasional noise and clucking of the tongue, there was nothing else to connect them to the house. It didn't even occur to him to check what she was doing.

As he stacked the cards, he raised his voice and called out, 'How about some tea?' When she appeared in front of them with cups of hot tea, he said with a smile, 'Today is a holiday. Why don't you make something for us to munch?' She nodded gently and left. She didn't get access to her chair the whole day. Nor did she have the time to sit on it. All her time was spent in making frequent cups of tea, breakfast and lunch. It wasn't at all like a holiday for her. It wasn't even a normal working day. It was constant, back-breaking work without even a minute's rest. All her expectations of spending the day with him had come to naught. The radio blared without any listeners.

She waited a long time expecting them to get up from the game but was disappointed. She didn't even have anyone to talk to. They seemed to have no intention of parting from the cards. They ate their lunch merely as an obligation, on the plank. Well before their wet hands could dry properly, they had picked up the cards. Whenever he moved in her chair, it screeched and summoned her.

Just like her, the chair too did not get a moment of respite. His old chair lay quiet, though. He had encroached on her chair little by little. He might even stake a claim on it, saying it belonged to him henceforth. He might even declare that it was already his. But she wasn't prepared to give up her chair. The wounds she had suffered to acquire it had not scabbed over yet. She wasn't such a duffer as to lose it so quickly.

As time passed, she felt more and more annoyed. Though it was well after sundown, they did not rise from the table. She had to get started on preparations for cooking dinner. But the outcry from her chair would not let her go. She got up suddenly. Catching hold of his hair, she lifted him and pulled out the chair from under him. She picked it up gingerly, like a baby with a soiled bottom, carried it to the kitchen and put it on the platform. He and the friend stood up, stunned. Then they sat on the floor and resumed playing. He never saw her chair again thereafter.

Translated from 'Isai Narkaali'

4

The Night the Owls Stopped Crying

Raju had taken up a job as a nightwatchman in a big farmhouse. The house was situated quite far outside the town. An elderly lady lived there alone. The servants employed to attend to her needs and take care of the farm went away at six in the evening. When Raju turned up fresh and bright in the evening, they waved him goodbye with a smile and headed home. Everyone called the old woman 'Amma', but Raju preferred to think of her as kizhavi (old woman) in his head. Amma had a servant to cook, wash clothes and sweep the house. There was a set of rooms inside the farmhouse which was almost like a separate flat. When Amma's relatives and close acquaintances came visiting, they stayed there. Some others too came on her son's recommendation and stayed for a few days, even paying rent for the accommodation.

There was a servant to look after that suite and the people who stayed there.

The farm was spread over an area of four acres. It was full of trees, mostly native species like neem, Indian beech, rain tree and jackfruit. There were a few coconut and papaya trees as well. They had cut off the lower branches of the trees, allowing them to grow to a great height. If one looked up, the foliage seemed like a cluster of nests high above. A servant came daily to tend to the trees and to mend the fences that enclosed the farm on all sides. If the old lady wanted to go out, a car was available. There was a man appointed to drive the car. He also had to undertake daily inspection of the doors and windows to make sure that no insects entered and no birds built their nests inside. This man was like the manager of the farmhouse. He hired the staff and disbursed their salaries.

After concluding negotiations with Raju, the manager took him to meet Amma. It was the only time he met her. Occasionally, she came out during the day and moved about. Now and again, people's voices and peals of laughter could be heard in the daytime; during the night, however, there was only the sound of dogs barking. There were four dogs on the farm and they roamed around the farm at all hours of the night. Raju didn't like them all that much. There was a cattle shed inside the farm for rearing cattle. At one time, there had been four or five heads of cattle in the shed. Now it was used for storing timber. There was a small tile-roofed cottage, which had once served as living quarters for the fellow who was looking after the cattle.

When Raju joined two months ago, certain conditions were conveyed to him. He too had put forth three conditions. He should be given a place to stay. He should be served food three times a day and tea twice. He should not be asked to do any work in the daytime. They had accepted all three without qualification and allotted the cattle-tender's quarters to Raju. It was a beautiful and well-maintained cottage. His possessions, which included four or five pieces of clothing, were very few. There was no disturbance to his sleep during the daytime. A nightwatchman couldn't find a more comfortable place to work in.

In all the years since he had run away from home, Raju had worked as a nightwatchman in many towns and in many types of establishments. When he started out, it was the only job he could get. Over time, he had grown used to the work and to the attendant routine. He had a very hard time during the inevitable gap of one or two days between leaving a job and joining another. He could not sleep a wink at night. He felt miserable, having to spend the entire night in his hovel of a room without sleep.

Because of his vocation, nights were familiar territory for him. He slept through the day. On most days, he did not get even a glimpse of daylight.

He thought that he did his work properly, without any shortcomings. But some unexpected problem would crop up suddenly, forcing him to change his employer. Since there was a perennial demand for nightwatchmen, he always got another job immediately. The only problem was accommodation. He needed a room where he could sleep undisturbed during the day.

He had grown used to staying awake at night. But it was impossible to meet and chat with people at night-time. He was forced to interact with men who did the same type of job and talk endlessly about the same boring topics night after night. Besides, he rarely saw any women. By the time he came out, the women would have reached home or were on their way. Anyway, he didn't have the time to stop and look at them. The occasions where he managed to talk to women were very rare in his life. A few words uttered by them on those occasions still rang in his years. Like picture frames, he had put up certain faces in his heart. Now and again, he would pick one and caress her to his heart's content.

When Raju went to his native village a few years ago, his mother spoke to him about his marriage. He indeed yearned for intimacy with a woman. But what girl would marry a man who stayed out all night and lolled at home during the day? No wonder his mother was still searching.

Raju loved listening to all kinds of sounds. He hated that hour in the night when all the noises died down gradually and everything became silent. When it happened, he would hum a song or bang hard on the ground with his stick. No sound could be a substitute for human voices. If someone spoke more than a sentence to him or listened patiently to what he was saying, he felt ebullient all night long. Most times, however, his routine was to walk along filthy city streets throughout the night.

On his rounds, he would see the trash piled up outside big office buildings, banks, warehouses and rich people's mansions, and dogs loitering in and around those piles. As the bustle of human activity dwindled steadily, the road assumed the visage of a corpse. A fetid odour started to waft at midnight. Milkmen and vegetable sellers brought the road to life at dawn. Even as the road became more and more alive, he took his leave. Why would anyone want to witness death from up close or leave the living behind?

The farmhouse was unlike the other places he had worked in. Leave alone women, he rarely saw another human being. It was a different world, with birds and towering trees, that was turning there. At six every evening, he turned on the lamps on all sides of the farm. Then he untied the dogs and set them loose. Similarly, at six in the morning, he had to turn off the lamps and tie up the dogs. He patrolled the entire farm throughout the night. The dogs were not of much use. Every now and then, they looked randomly in some direction, raised their snouts and started barking for no reason at all. If he ran forward and checked, not even a small dry leaf would have stirred there.

Once he realized that they were barking because, like him, they were weary of having nothing to do, he stopped giving any importance to it.

The farm was a large, rectangular expanse. Most nights, he would go and sit near the entrance on the eastern side of the farm. On a rare day, a vehicle might pass on the twenty-foot-wide road in front of the entrance. He would wonder for some time about where that vehicle was headed. He would listen keenly for any sound of the vehicle coming to a halt nearby. For him, it was like playing a game. If he walked in the other three directions, he would bump into fences. He had a torch that could send its beam quite far into the distance. Regardless of the side he was patrolling, he kept flashing the beam. There were snakes, he had been told. He didn't see any snakes. Unimaginably large field rats scurried across his path. Owls hooted, shattering the deep silence of the night. Their white wings marked with black lines and spots, the owls looked different from any he had seen before. When he first heard their cries, he was petrified by the sound. As he listened to it more and more intently, he grew to like it.

The sound they made was not gentle. Nor did

it start softly and become louder. It began at peak volume. It was like a child bawling immediately after being pinched. He loved those owls. He felt that they were like him. They stayed awake at night, unlike any other species of bird. But the owl was never alone. It was always with another owl, or more. Even if the cries were very loud, he was able to discern variations among them. And when they cried during copulation, there was a passionate tenderness in it. On hearing that cry one day, he had trained the beam of his torch up at a tree. He saw two owls leap off and fly away together. He felt bad about having spoilt their pleasure. He would have liked it if the owls lived closer to the ground. But the farm owner had cut off the lower branches of all the trees and let them grow to a great height. In the trees, the foliage at the top spread out like a tent. The owls liked to sit around there. He had to strain hard to see them. If they stayed lower down, he could talk to those owls too, like he did with parrots and pigeons. He considered the owl's cry a little companion that cheered him up every now and then.

Since the problem of food and accommodation was already sorted out, he was hopeful that his salary could be saved every month; with that money, he could look for a girl to marry. Once he acquired the gloss of money, relatives would seek him out to forge alliances. But his friend Sundaram, whom he met by chance the other day, told him something that nearly extinguished his hope. Raju had got to know Sundaram when both of them worked as security guards in two ATMs located right next to each other. Sundaram had trouble controlling his sleep. After one in the morning he would go inside and lie down. At such times, Raju was the guard for Sundaram's ATM as well. Sundaram had a soft spot for him. As soon as Raju told him that he was working in the farmhouse, Sundaram said, 'Isn't that place haunted?'

They had never appointed a watchman for that house. Once, not long ago, a gang of five men had brought a girl there, and raped and killed her before they went away. It blew up into a major scandal and the old woman's son had to come down from abroad to sort out matters. A nightwatchman was appointed only after that incident. No man who took up the job stayed there for more than a month. They stopped coming to work as soon as they were paid their salary for the first month. The girl who died was said to be roaming around the farm. 'Haven't you seen her yet?' asked Sundaram.

Raju spent that night in great fear and trepidation. Now the hooting of owls took on a different meaning. It appeared to herald the arrival of the girl's spirit; he avoided going to the side where their cries could be heard. But the owls cried by turns on all four sides. It seemed she was wandering across the entire farm. Dogs have the ability to see supernatural spirits. That was perhaps why the dogs on the farm barked looking in a direction from which no sound came. Sometimes, the four dogs barked together. He didn't understand why they should bark when there was nothing in front of them.

It was the end. He decided that he would wait to collect his salary for the month, and then leave suddenly and quietly.

How would he cope until then? There were more than fifteen days left. No matter which part of the farm he patrolled, he heard the sound of someone walking behind or alongside him. Though he guessed that it must be the echo of his own footsteps, it brought him no comfort. He stopped abruptly and shouted, 'Who is it?' His own voice echoed back. How could he spend every single night like this, in mortal fear? He had grown weary of his routine hitherto of patrolling one side and sitting there all night. Now he felt as if he had been infused with fresh energy. His ears hadn't lost their ability to hear even minute sounds, like the rustling of leaves, swaying of branches and the gentle splash of bird shit.

He tried to find out when the spirit arrived and in what form. When the dogs started barking, he peered intently in that direction. How wonderful it would be to have the eyes of a dog, he thought. God has given this fortunate gift for seeing formless spirits only to dogs. When he walked south at midnight, where everything looked frozen like stone statues nailed to the ground, a small whorl rose with a hiss from the boundary fence, moved slowly towards Raju, embraced him, floated a little further and subsided to nothing. He had not experienced the pleasure of such an embrace ever before. He felt as though the spirit had lifted his whole body in a tight clasp, let him float in the air for a brief while, then brought him down and left him on the ground. There was no need to fear this woman, he thought: she had given him great pleasure without doing him any harm.

During his daytime slumber after that encounter, dreams came to him in fragments. Normally he fell into deep, dreamless sleep. He had felt sad at times, wondering whether even dreams did not like him enough to visit him. As if to compensate for everything that had gone before, he had a plethora of dreams in a single day. Though he was unable to sort them out and relate them meaningfully to himself, he felt happy.

That night, he went to the same spot and stood there. Though he waited for a long time, no whorl turned up to visit him. He wondered whether it was the same spot where she had disappeared the previous day. Nothing happened till dawn broke. Didn't she like him? Though he had never looked in the mirror before, now he stood for a long time in front of the wide mirror in the bathroom of his cottage and scrutinized his appearance. The vitality of youth had not yet left his body. Was she averse to all men because of the men who had ruined her? How to make her understand that he was not that kind of man?

He put on some face powder. Pulling on a fresh shirt, he set out for his duty as nightwatchman. He waited until the same hour the whorl had passed him two nights ago and went to that spot. When she didn't turn up even after a long period of waiting, he shouted out to her: 'Come...why are you afraid of me? I won't do anything to you. Come here.' The dogs started barking. It wasn't clear to him whether the dogs were barking on hearing his voice or whether he had changed course and come to a different side of the farm. The dogs were familiar with his voice. In that case, he must have indeed changed course. He went in the direction of the barking dogs. There was nothing there. As he trudged dispiritedly through the farm, on the northern side a small whorl appeared suddenly and, as before, embraced him and disappeared. He began to address the spot where it had vanished.

He was surprised that he could so easily overcome his initial inhibitions about speaking to a girl. Even after the whorl had disappeared, he was able to see a faint, smoky figure. He realized that he too was endowed now with the special vision of dogs. As he walked, the figure too moved in step with him at a certain distance. When the dogs barked at her, he abused them using horrible words and brought them under control. Afraid that she might be put off by his anger and the words he used, he cut down on the abuse and gently chided the dogs. When she appeared to smile, he turned to her and smiled as well. Since she had caught on to his fakery in no time, he felt slightly ashamed. Once he started speaking normally to her, in spite of his gentle persuasion and encouragement, she refused to open her mouth, which left him feeling sad.

He didn't sleep properly that day, and lay brooding over her refusal to speak to him. He consoled himself by thinking, 'She is a woman, probably shy; she will get over it eventually.'

It would do if she came along, he said, and started speaking to her. He had plenty of things to say. Everything that had lain dormant within him for so many years came out spontaneously, without premeditation. His childhood years before he ran away from home were like the sandy expanse of a riverbed where joy flowed as if from a spring. Those years were full of endless incidents and people. Speaking about them brought a new vigour to his spirit. He was amazed at everything that had lain piled up inside that little child. Childhood must be full of joy for everyone, he said. He heard her muttering something in response. You can say that aloud, because there is no one here anyway, he said. He had restrained the dogs from barking at her. He had also trained them to wag their tail and pay her respect, just as they did with him. She muttered again. 'People are happy only during their childhood,' she said.

He lay in bed all day, reflecting on the truth and sorrow contained in her statement. As he pondered the mystery of how the joy of childhood seemed to seep out as a person grew older, he stumbled upon several insights and knots at the same time. Though he was dying to learn about her childhood, she simply wouldn't speak to him. Oh, she will tell me of her own volition, she has to, he reassured himself. 'Since childhood is joy itself, it endures in our memory; there are many ways for the joys of adulthood to disappear,' he said. He told her that the day after he ran away from home was the beginning of his adulthood; it was the moment when he took up the responsibility of making decisions about himself.

His father was the reason Raju had run away from home. Raju recalled how angry his father had been when he had gobbled up the egg in the egg kuzhambu that was reserved for his father, and the thrashing he received from the enraged man. He found it laughable. What a big joke it was that a single egg had changed the trajectory of his life. Overnight, it had changed his location and the people around him. Even small things are enough to bring about momentous changes, he stated philosophically and looked at her. He thought she might offer a correction that might be very meaningful too. Since she didn't say anything, he exulted in the conceit that he had said something she agreed with entirely.

When he left his village, he had had big plans. If he went to a big city, he would get a chance to act in films: not as an ordinary character, but a hero. In his village, he had seen plenty of films with money stolen from his father's pocket. What other qualification did an aspiring actor need? At that stage in life, it was natural for a person to imagine himself as a hero. There was nothing wrong in his ambition. But entering the film industry was like entering heaven. Plenty of doors had to be opened.

The average person couldn't even find where the doors were. So, he became a nightwatchman before too long, he told her.

What qualification did a nightwatchman need? The only condition was that he should not sleep while on duty. In his many years of experience, he had neither come across a thief nor caught one. But where did the popular belief that there were thieves everywhere come from? He didn't know. Now his nights went by in a rush. The farm was not big enough for his rounds. How lucky it was that in that desolate place only the two of them were present and awake. The dogs had stopped barking at her. The last time they barked at her, he had hit one of them, a big dog called Doo-doo, with his torchlight. From then on, he didn't hear even a small whimper from them.

He could do nothing about the owls, though. While he was describing something significant, an owl would cry all of a sudden. This interrupted his flow and brought it to a halt. By the time he recovered his earlier frame of mind and resumed the narrative, he'd be completely fed up. Since she found his embarrassment amusing, or so he thought, he never abused the owls. Holding that the owls had some primitive right to do so, he allowed the birds to come between them.

Meanwhile, when Raju ran into Sundaram one day, he asked Raju, 'Are you still working in that farm?' and expressed his surprise. 'Didn't the ghost do anything to you?' In response, Raju whispered in Sundaram's ear, 'I am the one who is putting a spell on her,' and laughed. Sundaram gave him an odd look and left.

Raju didn't feel frustrated at having to do all the talking himself. When he talked so much, the other person would be spurred to say a few things, right? But she limited herself to one or two sentences. Even that was by way of a brief opinion on, or correction to, something he had told her. She hadn't yet said a word about herself nor shown him her full visage. She continued to keep him at a certain distance. He had decided that he would never remind her of the calamity that had befallen her in the farmhouse. She could talk about other things, especially about the things that made her happy. He was also afraid that she might go away if he compelled her to speak. 'I don't like my father at all. How about you?' He angled for a response. 'Oh, I don't know who my father is,' she said, turning it into a joke. 'If you don't tell me something about yourself, I won't speak to you,' he told her peevishly. He realized that he had said it in a loud voice and with great passion.

It was only after he became conscious of his sweaty face and panting breath that he asked himself why he was getting so emotional about her. *What will I do if she stops coming here?* He became even more frightened. 'I'll tell you tomorrow,' she said. He was happy that his anger had borne fruit. He made her confirm several times that she would tell him the next day. So far, her voice had been a whisper. That he might hear the sweetness of it and get to know something about her, that she might talk to him face-to-face, gave him plenty of hope. In his eagerness, he kept babbling about something or the other until daybreak and then went off to sleep.

If he slept at dawn and woke up at nine, he would find his breakfast lying outside the door. After eating, he would circle the room for some time. If he went to sleep again, he would get up only at lunchtime. Even as he ate his lunch, sleep would weigh heavily on him. If he went to sleep again, it would be past four when he woke up. He would have just enough time to bathe and wash clothes. He turned on the first lamp exactly at six.

When he got up for breakfast the next morning, the manager was standing in front of his door. So far, there had been no complaints about his work. He couldn't fathom the reason for the manager's visit.

The manager came to the point right away. Amma had told him that over the past few nights she had been hearing human voices in the farm. She had dismissed it as her imagination. But she was taken aback last night when all of a sudden she heard someone shouting. She had opened the windows and seen Raju yelling and talking to himself as he ran past the house. She kept all the windows open and watched Raju's movements all through the night until dawn. If they employed a madman who talked to himself constantly, how could she live there without fear?

Do you want to work properly from now on, or do you want to leave, asked the manager. Raju stood quietly, saying nothing. The manager told him that they were going to hire a new watchman in a couple of days and that he had asked the cook to sleep over in Amma's room.

Raju didn't go to sleep after the manager's visit. He sat in his room for a long time. But the first lamp came on as usual at six. That night, Amma and the cook sat watching through the wide open windows. Raju's voice was not heard at all. The dogs barked as before. Contrary to their usual practice, the owls had stopped their crying.

Translated from 'Aandaigal Alaralai Nirutthiya Iravu'

5

An Unexpected Visitor

It wasn't daylight yet when the little old woman set out from the house, grasping her grandson's hand. The boy's face was flushed with sleep. He didn't know where Paati was taking him. He guessed it must be to some place new. All the places he had visited these two weeks of living in his grandmother's house were entirely new to him. They were places that he had never seen before, not even in his dreams. 'Where are we going, ayah?' He pestered her, asking the same question many times over. Paati lifted her short arm, pointed ahead and said, 'We're going there.' 'Where is *there*, ayah?' he asked her again, stamping his feet on the ground. 'There means there,' replied Paati. The exchange was like a game between them; it also helped them to continue their trek without feeling bored.

I'll find out anyhow, the boy decided, and shifted to a new game that involved running in front of and behind his grandmother. Whenever he grew tired of the game, he ran up to her, held her hands and asked in a beseeching tone, 'Where are we going, ayah?' He was used to knowing the journey's end and being prepared for it before setting out. Besides him, his parents too had done a lot of groundwork before coming to Paati's house. Paati alone seemed capable of going somewhere without any preparation whatsoever. Giving him some vague reply or just her toothless smile, Paati moved her hunched body at a slow pace and trudged along the foot trail that passed through and linked the fields.

Paati couldn't pronounce his name. So she called him 'Kunju' (meaning 'chickie' or 'little one'). Children of the village as well as elders made fun of that name by calling out, 'Hey, little one, the midget Paati's grandson.'

Chickie, chickie
Little chickie
Hen chickie
Crow chickie
Dry and salted
Fish chickie

Trouser clad
Towner chickie

When the boys crooned the ditty, Kunju would throw a handful of dirt at them and run back home. Paati was pleased that her Kunju had learnt so much in just a fortnight. She scooped up the cleverness from his face with both hands and rested it on her cheeks.

Kunju was not her grandson in fact, but her great-grandson: her granddaughter's son, child of her daughter's daughter. The daughter herself had passed away a few years ago, but the granddaughter somehow still remembered her grandmother. Most of the old woman's relatives had flown away in every direction like newly feathered chicks in search of prey. Whenever any of them visited the village on some occasion, happy or sad, they looked up Paati as well. Some pressed rupee notes into her hands. She did not depend on such gifts for her survival; arrangements were in place to provide her a monthly allowance. It was quite a generous amount for a solitary woman. Even so, she happily accepted the gift. If it made the giver happy, why should she spoil it? In Paati's fantasy everyone would come together to visit her one day. The whole village would gawk at them, amazed that she had so many relatives. When it happened, she might not even be able to see all of them. During sleepless nights, she would gaze at the sky and try to remember all the various branches of her network of relatives. She felt dejected if she was unable to remember someone's face. She did not rest content until she had somehow called up that face before her mind's eye. It was many years now since names had completely slipped from her memory.

Paati's body might have shrunk, but there was no let- up in the performance of her daily chores. Each day passed in a brisk routine of activity: cleaning the house and front yard, cooking, eating and bathing. When she sat on the front pyol and watched the street, there were so many scenes for her to witness. The human voices and activities that played out before her were a perennial source of wonder and amusement. Though she lived away from everyone, like a discarded object, someone or other passing by would provoke her deliberately with a remark or two. That would in itself become the old woman's biggest consolation for the day.

'Who are you waiting for, Paati?' Some young girl might ask just to make fun of the old woman. Earlier, if anyone asked her such questions, Paati's retort would be swift and sharp: 'Your husband has promised to come by this evening. That's why I am sitting here, waiting for him.' She would get it back too: 'Look at her! Our Paati is still as saucy as ever.'

But these days, she broke into a toothless grin and said, 'I am waiting for that Koothuvan to come.' 'You send the lord of death to all our homes while you sit here, solid as a rock. You must be the Koothuvan,' they teased her. Since there was some truth in that, Paati's face would wilt in sorrow. As someone who had witnessed countless deaths over the years, she would think sadly to herself: 'I am not refusing him, am I? For some reason, the Koothuvan doesn't seem to like me.' Brooding over the cruelty of the Koothuvan who seemed to be keeping away from her, she would lament within, 'Who knows what else fate has in store for me?'

One afternoon, when she was stretched out on the front pyol for a nap, her granddaughter, along with her husband and their boy, this Kunju, alighted in front of her from a motor car. She welcomed them, thinking that they might have come to the village on some other business and had dropped by to pay her a visit too. That she recognized them immediately and enquired about certain family matters pleased them enormously. When Paati went inside to bring them water to drink, she heard her granddaughter remark: 'As she gets older, the woman's eyes and ears seem to be growing sharper.' Kunju stood stiffly, with his eyes fixed on Paati.

It took Paati a few minutes to understand the reason for the granddaughter's visit. Both the young woman and her husband were office workers. Quite unexpectedly, both of them had to travel on work for a few days. It was summer vacation for the boy. So they had decided that Paati should look after the little one. Leaving him with anyone else was not an option.

If Paati could mind him for as long as she was able to, they would make some alternative arrangement in the meantime. They had two or three other places in mind. Worried that Paati might refuse, the granddaughter conveyed their proposal in a tone of abject pleading. Only then did Paati realize that she could still be of some use to others. 'Feel free to leave him here, ma. I'll look after him for even a month if necessary.' He was a six-year-old boy who had never lived away from his parents. His parents were visibly concerned that they were forced to leave their boy with an old woman. She tried to reassure them and instil some confidence in their minds. She grabbed Kunju's cheeks with her moist hands and held on to them. It made the boy squirm, but that touch was something he couldn't reject offhand.

'Kunju, Paati will buy you anything you want. This entire street is yours. You can play around here. There is a parrot chick in a tree that I'll get for you. Will you stay here with me?'

The expression on Kunju's face alternated between clarity and confusion. He had seen the figure of an old woman with wrinkles all over her body, sunken eyes and hunched back only as a cruel witch in cartoon shows. Although this old woman's appearance was very similar, he was confused by her voice which dripped affection and by the way she called him Kunju like no one else had done before. Besides, he couldn't understand much of what she said by curling her lips over her toothless gums. His father and mother had briefed him thoroughly before they brought him. If he acted stubborn, they would just leave him there, crying and screaming, and simply go away.

After handing over packets of snacks meant to last him for ten days and a big doll that looked like an overstuffed gunny bag, they pressed four or five large-denomination notes into Paati's hands. Looking alarmed and pained, the old woman asked her granddaughter, 'Why, ma?' She was troubled by the notion that she was being paid to look after her grandson. Only after the granddaughter told her, 'The boy will ask for all kinds of things. Please buy him whatever he wants, Ammayi. This money is meant for that,' did the old woman feel pacified. Reluctant to part from their son, the couple tarried, talking about this and that.

Paati had given birth to seven–eight children and raised them. One died within a few months of being born. She lost another at a very young age, when it was pulsing with life. This child came to her even now, clapping and laughing. It never grew up. It had danced and swayed as a child through all these years. She could no longer remember the childhood appearance of those who grew up and left in pursuit of jobs and other worldly things. She felt that it was this child, resident forever in her heart, who had come back as Kunju. Otherwise, why would a child come looking for her after all these years? Paati's body and mind gained a new strength and confidence.

Over the next two weeks, Paati never had a minute to stop and rest. With unwavering attention she fulfilled every one of Kunju's needs. He liked his food hot at all three meals of the day. Used to cooking just once for the whole day, Paati now had to cook a fresh meal three times a day. Paati was worried that her cooking might not be up to his taste, but he ate his food with relish. Since he was used to eating foodstuffs garnished with pungent masala powders, his palate was not familiar with the subtle tastes and flavours of Paati's cooking. She would add a dried chilli to cooked lentil and mash it to the consistency of scented water. Ridge gourd, greens, water gourd and aubergine – she would mash them all to pulp. He eagerly devoured her kuzhambus, thick gravies made with tamarind and lentil, in which the flavours of the vegetable were intact. She bought milk and made curd with it especially for the boy's consumption. He scooped up the thick curd with his fingers and licked it off his palm. Thus she was always busy with some cooking chore. Finding some time during the day for a brief shut-eye or just lying down became rare. Paati was scarcely aware of it, though.

Kunju woke up very late in the morning. Paati didn't feel like waking him up. He was usually fast asleep even after ten in the morning. She would finish cooking and sit staring at him, wondering whether he might wake up soon. Staring at a sleeping child would surely afflict him with the evil eye and she must perform the rite to avert it, she would tell herself. Concerned that sleeping on an empty stomach might affect his health, she would wake him up reluctantly. And she had to struggle hard to make him submit to a bath. Because there was no need for anyone to wake him up, quickly get him ready for school and cram him into the school bus, and because Paati never spoke a harsh word to him, Kunju was very happy staying in that village in the middle of nowhere. He would tuck into the food prepared by his Paati and run off to play.

In the street, a number of games would be in various stages of progress. He would join one of them. Once he started playing, he came to his senses only when Paati came to call him for his next meal. Paati would circle round the spot where he was playing and call out to him using many sweet words: 'Raja, Kunju...Kannu.' He acted as if he didn't hear her at all. Then she'd start pleading with the other boys who played with Kunju. No one from their homes came to coax them to eat. That wistfulness would turn into derisive laughter before they sent him off with her. Before he hurried home Kunju would promise them that he'd be right back after eating. He'd finish eating even before Paati returned home, and would run back to the game again. He played in the evenings too. The bag of playthings the granddaughter had left for him lay unopened.

After eating their meal at night, Paati and Kunju placed their cot outside the doorway and lay down on it. He would ask her to tell him a story. Paati had forgotten all the stories. Since it was many years since she had told them last, she struggled to bring them back to memory. Then she decided to tell the story of her own life. Kunju liked this very much. She recalled several incidents from her life and narrated them to him with a blend of wistfulness and longing. Everything that had lain frozen inside her began to thaw, and it poured out like a thick stream of treacle. Whenever Kunju raised a doubt, Paati did not scold him but responded with whatever she knew. As a result, Kunju asked her a lot of questions. Paati had completely forgotten the Koothuvan by now. She wouldn't recognize him even if he came in front of her. And if she did, she'd most likely chase him away, saying, 'Come back after a while.' Paati was experiencing the joy and happiness of her youth again.

Every day at eight, there was a phone call in a neighbour's house, just a short distance away from Paati's. Paati and Kunju would get there early and wait for the call. Paati had never spoken on the telephone. Kunju showed her how to use it. For the entire duration of the call, Kunju's father and mother took turns giving him advice. Even Paati received nothing but advice from them. They talked mainly about the ways in which she should look after him. Kunju said yes to everything they told him. Watching the boy, Paati learnt to respond in the same way. Until Paati finished speaking, Kunju held the handset of the telephone to her ear. Not once did Kunju ask his father or mother to come and see him. This, in particular, was a source of joy for Paati. When others teased her by saying, 'Now that her grandson is here, Paati has no time for anyone,' she was just as happy to hear it.

Kunju's activities did not stop on the street. He went along with other boys to roam the fields. A few boys climbed up palm trees to pluck palmyra fruit. They cut the shells open and gave some to him. He learnt to insert his finger, dig out the pulp and suck it straight from the shell. They wandered all over, looking for parrot chicks in the barren trees. It was scorching hot, but Kunju didn't stop roaming around. Paati couldn't go to the fields and look for him. After she finished cooking the afternoon meal, she sat at the doorway staring down the street, waiting for him.

One day, unable to tolerate the heat, he struggled even to chew his food properly and shouted in frustration. Paati was gripped by fear. She filled a bowl with watery gruel drained from a pot of cooked millet and made him drink it. Though he recovered a short while later, she didn't allow him to step out of the house the next day.

She was scared: how would she explain it to his mother if something happened to the boy? She didn't inform her granddaughter about Kunju getting heat cramps. Fearing that she might panic, Kunju and Paati concealed the fact from her. Paati was overjoyed; it was as if she had accomplished some major task with Kunju's help. The pleasure of doing something clandestine appealed to her even at her age.

Kunju spent the next day playing near the house. He was quite used to playing all by himself but the habit had left him after coming to Paati's house. While he played, he kept looking wistfully down the street. Unusually for him, he had a good nap in the afternoon. A few boys came by to ask, 'Kunju, aren't you coming to play with us?' Kunju simply couldn't bear to stay at home the day after. Promising his grandmother that he wouldn't go too far, he stepped out on to the street. Paati couldn't bring herself to be strict with him. It took him only a short while to revert into his usual self. He didn't go to the fields, however. Paati had to trudge to the spot where he was playing and bring him home for his afternoon meal. This routine was followed for the next couple of days.

On one of the following days, much to everyone's surprise, he slipped away to the well along with the other boys. During summer, the well invited everyone ardently, with its mouth wide open. Boys jumped into the well by turns from its many sides. Along with the din raised by practised swimmers, the fearful cries of learners as well as the joyful shouts of novices – who could swim a full circle around the well with a water gourd shell tied to their backs – were also heard regularly. Kunju sat on one side of the well mound and gazed fixedly into the well. He couldn't suppress the urge to get into the well and swim around. Given the general mood of frolic around the well, no one paid him any attention. If I could get hold of a water gourd shell, I can get into the water, he thought.

That night he pestered his grandmother for a water gourd shell. Paati was shaken to find out that he had even visited the well. The well exuded joy during summertime, keeping its cruelty well hidden.

When the cruelty was unleashed at the right opportunity, it crowed in triumph. Once in every two or three years, it would claim some young boy's life. While everyone swam around happily, it would gently drag some unsuspecting novice swimmer into the deep. During her lifetime, Paati had witnessed many such deaths. Whenever it happened, she would complain to the Koothuvan: 'Here I am, a ripe old log; instead of taking my life you've nipped a tender shoot.' She couldn't digest the fact that Kunju visited the well regularly. She knew the nature of the well. It would keep luring the innocent. Extending its phantom arms and using its seductive voice, it would entice those who visited it once to come back again and again. It was difficult for anyone to resist its appeal.

She could ask a responsible older boy to teach Kunju how to swim. She could also sit beside the well and keep a watch on him. She could narrow her eyes and keep staring at him. If he was in danger, she wouldn't be able to jump in and save him, but she could shout and raise an alarm. Back in the day, Paati had jumped into the well and splashed around even after marriage and a couple of children. But she was no longer that strong. Her muscles had lost their suppleness and she had turned stiff all over. When she stretched her fingers sometimes, she couldn't curl them back; if she flexed them, she couldn't stretch them out again. Though she was not robust enough to swim, her voice was still strong and clear. Her voice alone was enough to protect Kunju from any harm. But she was afraid of her granddaughter. The young woman who addressed her fondly as Ammayi, how would she take it if she knew that her son made regular visits to the well? And if she found out that he tied a water gourd shell to his back and splashed around, would she feel happy at all?

Paati told Kunju time and again that he must not go anywhere near the well. She pleaded with him to play only with those boys who didn't go swimming there. However, once the sun was directly in line with the forehead, all the boys in the village headed to the well. The well was crowded; so was the mound surrounding the well. What could poor Kunju do? Only after she was certain that she couldn't control him any more did Paati come to a decision. She felt the need for her had come to an end. The time to hand him over had come. She didn't know how she could repay god who had destined her, at her age, to be useful for a few days. Wasn't it true, as the adage went, that even a neem oil bowl, with its harsh smell and lingering bitter taste, could prove to be of some use?

As her granddaughter had told her, all she had to do was take Kunju and leave him in the house of another granddaughter on the outskirts of the city; she would safely hand over Kunju to his parents. Kunju watched eagerly as the sun rose like a red ball from a flank of the hill in the east. Stooping forward a little, Paati could only make slow progress. It had been many years since she had covered a long distance by foot. Normally, she went out of the house only to fetch water and to gather cattle dung for cleaning the front yard. She didn't even attend festivities held in the village. In her own house, she could sit with her legs stretched out, she could lie down and rest for a while. It might not be possible in other people's houses. If people came over on their own to give her the leftover sweets and snacks from the event, Paati didn't refuse them.

Watching the red ball gradually change colour, Kunju's delight knew no bounds. Empty fields, shorn from the recent harvest, lay sprawled before them. Straying from the foot trail that stretched in front of them like a lengthy piece of loincloth someone had thrown away, Kunju went galloping ahead. The early morning dew was a light damp in the air. Even as Paati kept shouting, 'Kunju, Kunju,' he ran whirling and dancing into the expanse. She was afraid that splinters might prick his feet. But she could not curtail Kunju's energy. A flock of mynahs that had descended on to the field rose with discordant cries and flew away. He saw a wonderful formation unfurl itself in the sky. He stood there, looking upward to see the magic of it shifting its shape every moment. Paati looked up too. It seemed to her as if some black dots were on the move. 'Whatever he sees is a miracle for our Kunju,' she observed aloud to herself.

She recalled the days when she had wandered all over these fields and dunes as a little girl. The memory made her face light up like a morning blossom. Kunju's presence seemed to bestow an enormous meaning to Paati's life of so many years. Kunju could stay on with her for a few more days. He could come and stay here during his later holidays. Would his parents let him, though? For that to happen, they should have some important work to do during every vacation of his. But why couldn't Kunju go to school from here? Paati did have the strength to stay with him and look after him. The dawn had stirred up an abundance of ideas inside her. Paati hadn't thought so much in recent times.

Why did Kunju have to come here? Why should he leave so soon? He hadn't asked to leave. His parents hadn't called him either. It was she who was afraid to keep him with her. Once she handed him over to the other granddaughter, her responsibility would be over.

The foot trail led to a fence and joined another that wound its way alongside the fence. Paati was breathless. As the sun climbed higher, walking would become more difficult. She sat down on a stone to rest. Kunju came running from the field. 'What is this, ayah?' he asked, wide-eyed. 'It's a fence, Kunju,' she replied. 'Where does it come from?' 'That's right. Where does it come from?' She hadn't thought of it in all these years. Where did this fence, covered by hill mango, nochi, neem and minna trees as well as thickets of morning glory, begin, Paati wondered.

She remembered many fields through which the fence passed. The fence wound on even beyond them. The next village, the one after that, and the one after that – the fence stretched out as far as she knew and continued further. She couldn't say where it began. 'It comes from there,' she pointed randomly in some direction. 'From where?' 'Beyond this village.' 'Beyond that, from where?' 'The next village.' 'Then?' Paati was exhausted from answering his questions. 'We'll walk there one day and find out.' When he asked, 'Does it go beyond the sky?' she pulled him towards her, sat him on her lap and said, 'Come here, my raja.' The lips that were squeezed out of her toothless mouth pressed softly on his cheek.

Freeing himself from her arms, the boy asked again, 'Where are we going now? Tell me.' With a happy expression on her face, she replied, 'We are going to your aunt's house.' Kunju stopped and turned abruptly, showing his back to her. He had most likely understood Paati's intention. 'Which aunt's house?' he asked. Paati had forgotten that granddaughter's name. She told him the name of the village. He too remembered what his mother had said at the time of handing him over to Paati: 'If you feel you can't manage, you can take him to the house of my aunt's daughter nearby. Don't you remember, Ammayi? She is the granddaughter of your daughter Araayi. You can leave him there. They have television in that house. He can spend his time watching it.' It was clear to him that Paati was going to take him to that house as instructed by his mother. He would be done with this village, then.

All of a sudden, he shouted, 'I'm not coming,' and ran headlong into the fence. Before Paati could stumble and rise, he had entered one of the many shortcuts through the fence.

'Kunju, Kunju!' Paati called out to him in panic. The fence was infested with snakes. Garden geckos and streaked lizards rambled through it. For bandicoots and field rats, there was no better habitat than the fence. In those segments of the fence covered by dense thickets, rabbits stood alert with their ears stiff and erect. If you were careless for even a moment, it meant the thorns in the fence not only tore through your clothes but also pierced the flesh. There were certain vines in the fence that posed a great danger. If you got caught in a tangle of such vines, freeing yourself was next to impossible. Paati was familiar with the fence since the time she was very little.

She was overcome by fatigue. She had walked a long way from home. Her eyesight grew dim. Kunju had disappeared inside the fence.

'Kannu, Kunju, Rasoo,' she called out to him. 'Paati!' his voice rang out with a laugh from inside a shortcut through the fence. His face was visible through a haze. As she called to him, 'Come, Kunju,' he ducked and wove through the shortcuts time and again and got away from her. His face appeared at the entrance to every shortcut. She couldn't do anything with him any more. 'Take me along too, Kunju. Let me also see where this fence begins,' Paati cried out as she walked so fast on the foot trail that passed alongside the fence that she was almost running, guided along her path by the sound of Kunju's laughter.

Translated from 'Veppenei Kalayam'

6

Mirror of Innocence

She wasn't the kind who woke up at midnight and disturbed everyone in the house. The child was usually asleep by eight or eight-thirty. She would wet the bed in her sleep. Her underwear and blanket, as well as the clothes of those sleeping beside her, would get drenched and stink of urine. But she never woke up. If any of them got up by chance during the night, they might take pity on the child lying soaked in a puddle, remove her wet underwear and change her blanket. She would sleep on, oblivious to it all. 'She is only two; she will grow up in a couple of years and get out of the habit,' they consoled themselves. It was only when she was troubled by persistent cough and cold that her mother would scold her – 'If you lie around in that puddle like a water buffalo, why wouldn't you catch a cold?' – and smack her lightly on the cheek.

But this child, who normally slept through everything, was putting them through an ordeal that night. Her cries had shaken them awake. It took them a few minutes to realize that it was the child who was crying. It sounded like the screeching of a bird whose neck was being squeezed. In the glow of the night lamp, they found her sitting up on the bed. Sleep had not left her face. She was crying steadily, without making a lot of noise.

'What happened, baby?' All three adults surrounded the child with anxious queries. 'What is it, da?' 'Why, ma?' 'What's bothering you?' Though they kept asking the same question in different ways, the child gave them no reply. Wailing was her only response.

As though an idea had just struck her, Paati went to her room and fetched a small tin of holy ash. 'Muruga!' she called out to her god as she applied a little ash on the child's forehead. She wanted to put a pinch of it in the child's mouth as well. 'Open your mouth, kannu,' she pleaded for a while, but the child refused to yield.

Paati went through the reasons why the child might be afflicted by evil spirits. 'Does she stay at home in the afternoons? She wanders here and there, playing all over the place at high noon, doesn't she? We tell her not to, but she won't listen,' she said with a sideways glance at her daughter-in-law.

'She might have seen something scary in her dreams, maybe?' suggested the child's father. 'Did you have a bad dream?' he asked the child, but there was no answer.

'She could be thirsty,' the child's mother said. 'Do you want some water?' she asked the child. 'Want to pee?'

Nothing drew a response from the child. The crying didn't let up. Seeing her weep with her mouth wide open, tears streaming down her cheeks, her mother burst into tears as well.

'She is ill, perhaps?'

Taking turns, each of them touched her forehead and neck to check for fever, but she wasn't running a temperature. Could it be latent fever, then? Their faces creased with anxiety, they tried to appease her with sweet words, then with biscuits and fruits, but to no avail. The child was too young to articulate what was bothering her.

Gradually, the bigger child's weeping threatened

to overtake the little one's. This annoyed the father even more. 'What's the point in crying and acting nervous at a time like this?' he asked his wife wearily, even as he kept his own sobbing and inner turmoil under control.

The mother asked gently, with a worried expression on her face, 'What do you want, my precious?' and placed the child on her lap. Rejecting her mother's fond embrace, the child kicked her legs and wailed even louder. Then she got down, sat on the bed again and continued bawling. When the mother brought her face close to the child's and asked in a cajoling tone, 'Tell me, kanna. What is bothering you?' the child relaxed her features as if making a generous concession and said, 'ip unda...aa...aa...' and became engrossed in crying once again.

They were relieved that they had somehow obtained a clue. They shot brief glances at each other. None of them knew the meaning of 'ip... unda'. Soon 'ip...unda' began to merge with the child's bawling as well. She intoned the phrase and followed it with a long-drawn-out wail, then it was 'ip...unda' again. The tears didn't stop, however.

'What is it, ma?' 'What is bothering you, ma?' Though they continued to ask the same questions, 'ip...unda' was the only reply they got. Even as they remained stumped over the meaning of the term, the child expanded its response to 'Ip...unda...I want.' It seemed like she was asking *for* something. What could it be? What precious object could wake her up in the middle of the night and induce a ceaseless crying tantrum? Had anyone taken it from her and hidden it somewhere? Was she recalling an incident from that morning when the boy from the neighbouring house might have snatched it from her and run off home? Even then, what was so precious about it that she had to ask for it, screaming and crying, so late in the night?

The two women recalled all the objects the child had played with, speculated on the meaning of 'ip...unda' and asked the child about specific objects. She usually played with a set of miniature wooden toys. Was it a cup from the set or a glass marble? The child rejected each suggestion with an emphatic 'hmm' and again cried out, 'I want ip...unda.'

How could the two women not comprehend her language, in spite of spending all their waking hours with her? What could the father do, anyway, except vent his frustration on them? 'So neither of you can figure out what it could be?' he asked, visibly annoyed.

'Yes, your child will ask for random things and being informed about them is our only job,' his wife retorted.

The father wondered if he should forget about the child and pursue this battle with his wife. He chose to console himself with a mumble under his breath: 'What other job do you have, then?' The burning sensation in his sleep-deprived eyes spread to his mind. He was afraid that with the child's continuous bawling, he and his wife might end up clawing at each other. He could sense that every glance exchanged between them was a preparatory step towards that nasty row. He felt a terrible headache coming on. He closed his eyes and leaned against the wall. Like the relentless buzz of a fly in his ear, the child's wailing drilled into his head. This checking off of random objects one by one could go on till sunrise.

Foreclosing that possibility, the magic object surfaced in her consciousness suddenly. God himself must have descended on her tongue. 'Was it uppu kundaạn, kannu?' she asked. 'Hmm,' the child affirmed with a nod and resumed chanting the magic words again.

The mother's heart swelled with pride at having been the one to discover that the object was indeed their salt bowl. Her face shone brighter than the lamp. She translated the child's speech for the father. Salt meant sugar. Since there was no visible distinction between salt and sugar, the child had adopted salt as the single name for both. She was referring to the small bowl that was used to scoop salt – that is, sugar – as 'uppu kundaan' (salt bowl). If they found the uppu kundaan and gave it to her, the crisis would come to an end. The father could sleep in peace. Still, the fatigue and inflamed eyes he would have to suffer the next morning frightened him.

The mother said with some diffidence: 'I gave her the kundaan to play with yesterday. Don't know where she threw it.' Where should they look for it? The child could have played with it anywhere.

Why would she give kitchen utensils as playthings to a child, the father fumed. He wanted so badly to slap his wife that his face turned red with anger. Provoked further by her irresponsible act and the child's endless crying, he snapped, 'Go and look for it somewhere.' His voice betrayed extreme frustration and anger. His wife didn't say anything.

'She was playing in the house. Where could she have tossed it?' Paati asked. All the lights in the house were switched on. The search mission began in earnest. They looked first in the cardboard box where the child hoarded all her playthings. Along with her toys there were a few twigs and torn pieces of paper, safely hidden. If it was daytime, the child wouldn't have allowed anyone to touch her treasure. Now she cared about nothing except that 'ip...unda'. Her stubborn wailing would have made anyone surrender to her will. If she was thrashed, it would only make her even more obstinate.

The father didn't know anything about the bowl. He had never had the good fortune of casting his eyes on it, because it was normally buried inside the sugar tin. To stop the child's wailing, he searched in all the spots he could think of. To facilitate his search, his wife described the shape of the bowl to him again and again. *It was made of lead. It was only as wide as one of those small earthen lamps, and around five centimetres in height. There was a small fissure near the mouth.* It was to get hold of this miracle object that the child stayed rooted to the same spot, doing this penance. When the father attempted to wipe the phlegm trickling on to her mouth from her runny nose, she flailed her hands, squirmed and resisted stubbornly. He wondered about the object she might have stashed inside that bowl.

They had looked in all the lit spaces. How had it disappeared, as if by magic? Now they had to extend the search to the deserted street where dogs lay asleep. The wailing didn't stop. How did that thin body have the energy to cry for such a long time with no discernible lowering of the pitch? The father was amazed.

Somewhere, a cat mewled like the child. At any other time, they would have been startled by the untimely whimper, but they were wide awake now as if it was afternoon. Frustrated at failing to find the bowl, the mother twisted the child's ear and shouted: 'Why are you so stubborn? Is it the time to cry and throw tantrums? Where have you gone and dumped the damn thing?'

Her outburst didn't strike the father as reproachable. His frustration had been growing as well. He wanted to grab hold of the child's bald head and dash it against the wall to assuage his anger. He made an effort to recover by telling himself over and over again, 'She is a child, after all, just a child.' He tried to deflect his impatience by reminding himself that the child wasn't ill. Had that been the case, they would have had to trudge from one street to another in the middle of the night, knocking on the front doors of doctors' residences. On top of that, they would have experienced nerve-wracking anxiety about what the child could actually be going through. Since the present situation was not so grave, he instructed his mind to remember that fact and remain patient.

It was Paati who spoke up to protect the child: 'Poor thing. She is sleepy. Don't beat her now.' One became more compassionate and patient as one grew older, perhaps.

What made the child remember the bowl now? Would she have dreamt that some thief was running away with it? Didn't god send beautiful angels to the dreams of young children? Might the child have stashed the loving gifts presented by the angels in that bowl? Was it the most invaluable object among the child's cache of playthings? Why was this particular bowl so close to her heart? What could be the reason? If those very angels found the bowl and returned it to the child, everyone in the house could go back to sleep peacefully. The father felt a twinge of regret that he didn't know the magic words with which to summon those angels.

They got hold of a flashlight to search in the corners where the electric lights couldn't reach. As time went by, the intensity of the child's wails increased instead of subsiding. The father sat down involuntarily, as if in the grip of a hallucination. The child's mother and grandmother seemed set to turn the entire house upside down in their search for the missing bowl. Sleep weighed heavily on the father's eyelids. By then he had become inured to the sound of her crying. He felt that he could doze off while the sound was still ringing in his ears. His mind had become serene.

Sensing his state of mind, his wife told him,

'Relax and go to sleep,' and even as she said it, her hands found the salt bowl, in the little space between the grinding stone and the wall it was placed against.

'Here's your salt bowl.' She held it out to the child. The emphasis she laid on 'salt' contained a touch of pride and joy. Having found it herself, she also felt relief, as if an enormous burden had been lifted off her shoulders. No one could blame her any more.

The father took a look at the bowl. It was an ordinary lead bowl. Even a junk dealer wouldn't buy it.

The child received the bowl as if it was made of gold and lay down immediately. Her wails morphed into gentle sobs, which began to die down as well. Closing her eyes, she gradually sank into deep slumber.

Translated from 'Peridhinum Peridhu'

7

The Goat Thief

A minor slip occurred in Boopathy's plan. To silence the goat, his fingers clamped its tongue without getting caught in its teeth, but his grip slipped a bit. Adjusting his grip, he tried to choke its vocal cords. In the meantime, the goat opened its mouth with its quaking tongue and raised a lone bleat. Confident that the sound couldn't have penetrated the darkness, banged on the dew-stiffened door and roused anyone from sleep, he hugged the goat to his chest and lifted it. It was somewhat heavy. The next moves of the goat – leaping and kicking to free its legs – were familiar to him. The way he held the goat gave no room for such manoeuvres. One hand was thrust inside its mouth, while the other held the animal tight against his body. *From now on, everything will go according to plan.* He walked rapidly towards the foot trail, landing his bare feet gently on the ground.

'Who is that?' He had gone barely twenty feet when he heard the commanding voice, along with the rustle of palm leaves behind him. He recognized the owner of the voice, and more people were beginning to join him. Boopathy couldn't decide whether he should drop the goat and flee or keep running with the goat on his shoulders. He came to an abrupt halt. Before his pursuers' eyes got used to the darkness and they started chasing him, he could cross the dirt trail and reach the road. Murugesan, who was waiting there on his moped, could ride so fast that he would cover a mile in the time a man tried to sit on the pillion. But if Boopathy ran with the goat on his shoulders, the noise would make it easy for his pursuers to nab him. He had never been in such a predicament before.

'Appov...our goat is missing!'

Boopathy trembled when he heard the agitated cry. He would be finished if they laid hands on him. He dropped the goat immediately. Its tongue set free, the goat let out a scream. It was the primordial cry of an innocent animal stunned at being dropped like a rock on the ground. But Boopathy had run a fair distance by the time its cry fell on his ears. The bustle of men moving about and the barking of dogs had begun to come together at various spots. He sprinted, thrusting his body forward like a stone aimed at a tamarind pod by a boy. The sound of his feet thudding on the ground pounded in his ears. He also sensed someone running not far behind him. Turning back to look would slow him down.

The dogs in the neighbourhood barked in unison. Boopathy's earlobes tingled with fear. 'Thief, thief!' 'Catch him!' He heard them scream in the distance as though from inside a well. All he had to do was reach Murugesan, who stood ready near the culvert with the engine of his soundless moped running. Boopathy sprinted single-mindedly towards the culvert. When his feet touched the pits on the tar road, they bounced and leapt. In the light of what he was able to see in the familiar darkness, he figured that he could catch up with Murugesan in four or five leaps.

With the goal so near, he tried to coax his legs to run faster. Just when he was feeling confident of jumping on to Murugesan's pillion in one more leap, a hand fell on his nape, pulled him back and pushed him hard. Tottering on unsteady feet, he was about to fall down. By now, Murugesan's moped would have travelled so far that no one could have gone after him. Before his pursuer came back from vainly chasing Murugesan's vehicle, Boopathy had recovered and assessed his situation. Both sides of the road were blocked. The men and their dogs had brought the road to life. Only the two ends of the culvert were still free.

He jumped into the torrent of sewage water that came swirling down the gutter. His legs sank in up to his knees like in the watery slush of a paddy field; drawing them out quickly, he took another step and waded in. The channel was wide and capacious. There was a lush growth of sedge grass and thorny babul trees all around. He could hear the sound of water swirling under the culvert. Boopathy entered the thicket of sedge grass and forged ahead. It was unlikely that any movements of the grass would be visible in the darkness from far away.

As soon as Boopathy jumped into the water, the fellow who was running after him stopped in his tracks, stunned. 'There he is, there he is,' he shouted and clambered on top of the culvert. 'Come on, da! Come fast,' Boopathy heard him calling out to the others. Boopathy had come very far inside the canopy of sedge grass. Raising a din, the men and their dogs surrounded the channel. Boopathy thought it might be wise not to risk any further movement. In the middle of that patch of sedge grass as tall as a man, he found a lone, sharply angled stone jutting out of the water. He climbed on to it and sat down. His legs were shaking. The slush and the water had drenched his body up to his waist. Sweat poured from his head on to his torso, making him feel as if he was just out of a bath.

Meanwhile, his pursuer was explaining the situation to everyone. Flashlights shone their beams inside the grass canopy. A large crowd of people had collected next to the culvert. There must have been thirty–forty people in the crowd. Some carried sticks in their hands.

The darkness would not betray any movements inside the sedge grass. If he walked further inside the canopy, he would reach the sluice gate of the lake. If he walked towards the banks, he would reach the coconut grove with a mud wall around it on one side and a sand track that led to the lake on the other. The moment they sighted any movement in the grass, someone might get into the channel aiming for that spot. He would not be able to sit for too long on that small stone. The soles of his feet were inflamed.

Amid the thickets of sedge grass he saw what appeared to be a sand dune. He got down from his stone perch and moved towards it. It was indeed a sand dune. A thorn bush had covered most of the mound. His feet stepped on a tangle of sharp, rough things. He took out the penknife tucked in at his waist and gently snipped away the thorny branches extending at ground level. The clearing held just enough space for him to lie on the ground. He lay down on his side. If he turned over on his back, the thorns would hover dangerously close to his eyes. If he stretched his legs, his feet would touch the water. He somehow curled up and lay in that narrow space. Nothing moved anywhere.

Now he could hear the voices from beyond the channel. Darkness added to the clarity of sounds.

Even a light rustle made his earlobes stiffen with fear.

'He couldn't have got away. He must be hiding somewhere inside this gutter.'

'He was moving so fast that he may have reached the lakeside by now, scrambled ashore and made a run for it.'

'If a man entered this gutter, he must have been ready to risk his life.'

People milled about on all three sides of the channel. Flashlights swept the area relentlessly. Boopathy was sure that none of them would find him. He was at the centre of the channel, surrounded on all sides by the tall thickets of sedge grass. From a distance, his hiding spot wouldn't be visible under any amount of light. The engulfing darkness would make it seem as if the spot too was filled with sedge grass. What would he do if four or five robust youths like him dared to jump into the gutter to nab him? His imagination was running wild.

Just when he had nearly stopped perspiring, more beads of sweat appeared again. He appealed to his clan deity. 'Amma...Kariakali...save me, Mother,' he mumbled to himself. He didn't know what else he should pray for. Closing his eyes, he kept repeating 'Kalimma, Kalimma' like an incantation.

The chatter of voices kept getting louder and louder. The hour was past midnight, with its unique blend of darkness and dew, but everyone wanted to stay back and watch the fun. If the incident had involved merely the theft of a goat, it would have ended up as just another bit of news. Now it had grown into a topic on which interesting gossip could be exchanged for a few more days. He heard all kinds of voices now, including those of women and children. Boopathy's ears grew erect, like a dog's. First he heard the sound of stones falling like rain inside the sedge grass. Then the abuses began and flowed freely: 'Come out, motherfucker!' Anticipating that a stone might fall on him, Boopathy curled his body further into a ball. However, not a single stone landed anywhere close. Like palm fruit falling from the tree, they kept dropping into the slush with loud thuds. He was far enough away that he could not be approached by man or stone.

Even after dawn broke and daylight spread everywhere, no one would be able to find him if he remained in that position. Boopathy felt strong and confident again. The sound of stones falling subsided gradually. The crowd didn't seem to know what to do next. People made all kinds of suggestions. The owner of the goat kept describing his adventure to many people. He ended his narrative always with the same lament:

'I missed him by a whisker. I had pulled him back and flung him on the ground. If only I had caught his throat immediately, he couldn't have escaped. Instead I went after the guy on the vehicle...this one had recovered by then. How was I to know that he would jump into this stinking gutter and get away so fast, as if he was swimming in a well?'

The flashlights continued to scan the sedge grass with their beams.

'Dei, none of you can pluck even a pubic hair of mine. Come here, da, if any of you has the guts.' As he became conscious of his mouth muttering the challenge, Boopathy chuckled to himself.

A woman said wearily, 'The goat is safe now, right? So why are you people loitering around in this cold? That man who entered this filth, do you think he will still be there? How do we know where he climbed ashore and in which direction he took off. The darkness is piled so thick that you can hack it slab by slab. Go and get on with your work.'

'Why don't you go home if it bothers you? How could a thief dare lift a goat from the doorway of a house? How can we rest without finding out what his face looks like? Even if we have to wait here till sunrise, we won't go home without catching him,' declared an energetic voice. 'Someone go and bring a fire torch,' commanded another. He could hear the bustle of a few men leaving. 'We have to go to work in the morning. Feeling very sleepy now.' A few women and girls seemed to be leaving for their homes as well. He didn't understand why they needed a fire torch. For a moment he was afraid that they might close in on him using the torch. 'Let them come. I'll see what they can do,' he thought boldly and stretched his legs. By now, the spot had become comfortable for stretching out. A few stars were visible in the sky through the gaps between the thorns.

'Ei, Marappa...keep a watch on that side. He might head for the lake over there and climb on to the bank and run away. The boys have gone to bring a fire torch. We'll wait for them to come.'

A message was sent from the sand trail side of the channel to the coconut grove side, which had very few men standing by; on the grove side there was only a foot trail, formed over time by villagers visiting a nearby field to defecate. No one could stay there for too long. He could clamber up over there, he thought. He postponed thinking about what would happen next and preparing himself for it. No trace of anger could be detected in the voices any more. Now they were mostly relating stories about the many cattle thefts that had taken place in the area earlier. Boopathy realized that a few of those had been carried out by him.

It was his father who had trained Boopathy in the art of stealing goats. Boopathy often felt that his own exploits were next to nothing compared to his father's. His father had never been trapped like he was right now. No man had waited with a vehicle to help his father get away. The goat across his shoulders had never made the smallest sound regardless of the distance it was carried. His father had told him about the most suitable hours of the night for stealing a goat – the time when Yama, the Lord of Death, having beaten all living creatures to sleep, played about freely: from midnight to three in the morning. Even old people and chronically ill patients shut their eyes during those hours. The period is a boon granted to us by god, Boopathy's father had told him often. 'Our actions must always be free of anxiety,' was one of his father's prime lessons. He had also taught Boopathy the technique of holding the goat's tongue as well as the knack of lifting the goat to one's shoulders.

The inaugural theft of Boopathy's career was carried out in the house of a frail old woman. She lived alone with two goats in a thatched shed in a field. One was a white male goat that had been castrated at the right age and the other was a black female kid. White goatskin fetched a lot of money. If there were two targets in one place, he had to choose the one that would earn him more income. This was also a lesson he had learnt from his father. He aimed for the ram. But he felt a qualm in his heart. Should he rob a lonely old woman of the fruit of her labours?

'There's hardship in everyone's life. If we start worrying about that, we'll never be able to practise our trade. Better keep *our* hardship in mind,' his father had said. Boopathy considered it no great achievement on his part to have stolen that goat. His hold was perfect. The old woman did not suspect him at all. His legs trembled, however. The trembling didn't stop even after he had brought the kid home. Still, he felt that his mind was strong. It seemed like all his fears had descended to his legs. After that first job, everything became easy and routine.

There was nothing special about holding the goat's tongue and lifting it to one's shoulders. Observing the daily routines followed in the target house before the theft was much more crucial. It was gathering intelligence on the various aspects – the shed where the goats were tethered for the night, the easiest way to get there, the distance between the shed and the house, the number of residents in the house, the spot where each resident slept daily, the person who had trouble sleeping – that required a lot of effort and legwork. One had to put on many guises, like a customer at the local toddy shop or a trader who bought and sold calves of water buffaloes and bulls. If everything was calculated properly in advance, the theft at night became easy to pull off. Before the owner of the goat even realized that the goat was missing, its meat would be cooking in many houses in the area.

After Boopathy teamed up with Murugesan, the work became even more of a breeze. Murugesan would ride his soundless moped stripped of its lights in pitch darkness. Once Boopathy got on the pillion with the goat, no one who came after them could catch them. Murugesan often said that it was best to practise moderation in everything. Once a goat was lifted and brought home, there must be a gap of at least one week before the next job. From the site of one theft to the next, there must be a minimum distance of ten kilometres.

Sometimes Murugesan too suffered a bout of enthusiasm, coming up with a host of daring ideas. Once, after they had handed over a stolen goat to the owner of a meat stall in the bazaar and collected the money, the butcher told them: 'I couldn't buy a single goat today. It's a festival day in most villages around here. If I can get another goat, it would be great. I am willing to pay fifty or hundred extra.' What could they do when it was already four in the morning? For stolen goats, the butcher always paid a fair price without haggling. He was a long-standing customer. If they brought him a goat, he slaughtered and skinned it immediately, regardless of how many goats he already had in his yard. Murugesan told Boopathy, 'We have to somehow help our man, pa.' He borrowed a vehicle from the butcher himself. It was a noisy machine fitted with lights. 'I'll try my best. After that, it's your luck,' Murugesan told the butcher.

He stopped the vehicle in front of a house on the outskirts of a village. A woman was milking goats in the cattle shed. Murugesan couldn't see her face in the dark. He went straight to her and said, 'Ammov, I've come to collect the goat.' He untied the goat and brought it to her. As she continued milking, the woman said, 'Take out the tethering peg and keep it on the floor before leaving.' He pulled out the peg, placed it on the pyol and said, 'I've done it, Ammov.' It was believed that if a goat was sold along with the tethering peg, its progeny wouldn't survive.

'I'll come by at ten. Tell Natrayan that he should hand over the cash,' the woman shouted. 'You'll get the money at ten sharp, Ammov,' Murugesan shouted back as he lifted the goat, kept it across his legs and sat on his vehicle.

The goat had already been sold to one Natrayan, who had promised to collect the goat that morning. When Murugesan and Boopathy went to the house, the woman had mistaken them for Natrayan's servants. The theft was discovered only when Natrayan's man went there after sunrise to take possession of the goat.

'You should listen keenly to everything that falls on your ears. After all, even a neem oil bowl may come in handy for some purpose,' Murugesan told Boopathy.

But so far, even Murugesan hadn't faced a situation like the one he was in. If this mob got hold of a thief, they would tear his limbs apart. After they were done with his body, he could only beg on the streets to survive. That was why Boopathy always packed a small knife in the knot of his lungi. He would be able to at least nick his adversary and get away.

Two or three fire torches were visible from his hiding spot. Those men might enter the grass thickets in the gutter holding those aloft. If they did, he would be forced to shift to another spot. Like a tadpole, he could find some nook or gap to hide in. If he crawled slowly across the channel, he could climb on to the opposite bank and take off. But no one entered the channel. Using the torches, they set the dry patches on fire. The fire didn't catch easily. Dampened by the dew, the reeds went out fast. After that, the men lost all interest in the chase.

'Let's go, da. This guy will surely get bitten by snakes.'

'Anyone who steals to survive deserves to die like that.'

'He will lie there all night with the thorns pricking his skin and die of the poison. We'll come in the morning and fish out his corpse.'

'There must be shards of glass in that sewage water from god knows where. Surely they will cut into his legs? Scavenging dog. Instead of lifting goats for a living, he should pimp out his mother.'

After delivering lethal curses, the crowd began to thin out. All the curses of hate and intolerable anger flung at him seemed to melt away in the wind. Why so many curses for a theft he couldn't even pull off? He chuckled softly to himself. He closed his eyes. The crowd's chatter decreased gradually until it sounded like whispers from the road. From their voices, he could make out that even the couple of men left on the coconut grove side were moving away.

Playing a trick on him, a few men could still be hiding there. The moment he became visible, they might pounce on him and nab him. The owner of the goat had been somewhat bold. He had followed Boopathy without worrying that his adversary might be carrying a knife. The owner's hold and push still lingered on Boopathy's body. He decided not to get up from his spot for the time being. He had no option but to wait for everything to die down completely. Sleep weighed heavily on his eyelids and wore him out. Though he had instructed his eyes not to give in to sleep, they were in no mood to obey. But he was a light sleeper at night: if his head slumped just a little, he would wake up.

When he woke up finally, he could feel the wetness of the dew all over his face. He could not get up immediately. Thorny branches covered him like a blanket. The dried slush on his legs pulled sharply at the skin underneath. Moving his feet even a little was hard. He looked at the sky. Sirius, which deceived the eye by glowing exactly like the morning star, glittered in the low sky. He estimated the time to be around four. He crawled horizontally and came out of the net of thorns. As before, it was pitch-dark all around.

He could hear the strange sounds of unfamiliar insects. It was as if his ears, blocked until now, had opened up suddenly. He heard a rhythmic, deep-throated gurgle, which could have been a frog's croak or something else. He wondered if it could be the secret language of snakes. As far as the eye could see, the channel was covered with sedge grass. The reeds stood taller than a man. Who knew what dangers lurked inside those grass thickets? He jumped down from the sand dune and climbed on to the stone. He should not go back the way he had come. He had to find some other route. He looked around. Towering over the sedge grass, the thorny branches of the babul trees looked like skeletons. His eyes met the same spectacle on all sides.

Deciding to walk towards the coconut grove, he took the first step. His feet sank deep in the tangle of roots beneath the grass. His legs were buried in the mud up to the knees. He was frightened. The noise of insects around him seemed to grow louder. He tried to pull his legs out. He felt each leg rise, then sink again. He reached for the stone and held on to it. Pressing down on the stone with his hands, he lifted both his legs out of the slush. When he sat on the stone again, he felt enormously relieved. Though the dew still felt cold on his skin, he began to sweat.

He was trapped in a patch of quicksand from which there would be no escape. The curses flung at him by the men had turned into the sedge grass, thorns and quagmire that confronted him now. Was this not the way he had come in? How could the grass reeds, which had parted for him then, close up now? His legs began to shake involuntarily. It was the same trembling he had experienced when he had lifted the goat from the old woman's house that first time. He tried to shake off the tremors like they were slush on his feet and gather courage.

He looked at the sky. The morning star was twinkling like a yellow sapphire. His time was up. Now the bustle of human activity would begin.

He heard voices from some place far away. The grass reeds around him had turned into human shapes that screamed at him. The thorn trees had morphed into men who stood before him with their arms stretched wide to catch him. All the various sounds merged into a giant scream: 'Thief! Thief!' He felt a surge of anxiety. His legs began to leap forward.

Translated from 'Velli Meen'

8

Shit

It was a fine-looking tumbler. Even though the years have passed, it hasn't faded from my memory. It was a plastic one, with a light brown lower half and a white upper half. When it was filled to the brim with beer, it looked like a pregnant woman. Elegantly shaped and almost weightless, it was easy to hold and handle. Like a wasp burrowing through those happy times, its giant shape adorns my dreams. Whenever the quantity of beer in the tumbler goes down, a bottle suspended in mid-air fills it promptly to the brim. The purple of grapes, pale yellow and amber, the black of a cave spring. The liquors blend together, creating a chaos of colours. A subtle variation in the sound as the liquor is poured, the discordant slosh when it falls into the tumbler. The liquor turns into a hard crust. When the tumbler overflows, the crust wriggles like a worm and spreads across the rim.

The stickiness of attachment. The liquor in the tumbler has a stink that ruins the fragrance of your dreams. It crams the stink into your mouth, spits it out through the nostrils and smears the stench on the organs. It flows along with your nervous sweat when you are startled awake, and spreads unremittingly on your skin as you keep wiping it off.

The spot where the tumbler sat is clearly visible now: at the back of an old house, in a corner by a wall that is obscured from sight, all alone. Covered by filaments of cobwebs, it trembles lightly in the breeze. With the release of a tense sigh begins a story.

~

In those days, we stayed in a remote suburb of the city. The house we lived in had many rooms and an inbuilt magic. The five of us – who were bachelors but not quite celibates – scarcely knew how to make proper use of those rooms. We preferred to loll around as we pleased. Our meagre possessions lay scattered across all the rooms. Trash accumulated in the house in a myriad of unexpected ways. Our house was made liveable only when some good woman swept the house every day and took out the garbage morning and evening. The house was so big and spacious that it took a few seconds for us to grasp who exactly was speaking from which room. Its wide windows opened to a view of the surroundings. Laden with flowers like white specks, overgrown parthenium shrubs peeked in from everywhere. A stretch of two or three large vacant plots lay between the house and its nearest neighbour. We were content to roam within the confines of the house. We neither felt the urge to inspect the surroundings nor harboured any perverse desire to breathe in the open air. The expansive freedom of those big rooms was enough for us.

To meet the requirements of the day whenever one of us came by a few high-value currency notes, we had equipped ourselves with a water jug and a few tumblers. Our voices rose in the night resembling the howls of wild animals, but they faded away in the open without reaching anyone's ears. We were fortunate to have this wonderful freedom to satisfy the legitimate urges of our youth.

We had conducted many inconclusive debates under the cool light of a green bulb, often in a wobbly state of intoxication. When the violent urge to tear into one another got out of hand, it led to shouting, weeping and physical assault. Our house was the arena where many different ideas animated by concern for society clashed furiously with one another. All of us had solutions for everything, and the starting point of our debate would always be about which solution was appropriate. As the heat of the debate mounted, we babbled more and more and struggled to speak coherently. At such times, fancying ourselves as divine incarnations, all of us reached for the speaker's throat with our hands, intending to snuff out his voice. On normal days, we barely had the time to sit and have a leisurely chat with one another.

When someone eventually realized that the pile of trash had grown even bigger, he would clean up the house if he could spare the time. When the trash was swept, gathered and scooped up, stinking dead frogs and house rats were found in it. The droppings of house lizards would have collected in a corner. Bare skeletons of charred cockroaches and house crickets lay in a pile. 'Adengappa, we seem to be cohabiting with so many different creatures,' we laughed and joked among ourselves. We marvelled at the thickness of our nostrils, which couldn't be penetrated by the stench from the carcasses.

Now and again, a cat appeared from nowhere and jumped in through a window, clutching a prey. A garden lizard or field mouse or birdling would be writhing in the deathly grip of its teeth. It entered the house, moved casually to a corner of its choice and settled down to consume its prey with slow deliberation, licked its chops, opened its mouth in a wide yawn and then went away. Our house was a suitable haven where it could eat its prey without disturbance. The remains discarded by the cat were strewn in the corners of several rooms. The foul odours from those remains never bothered us much either. 'Why make a fuss about the stink in our house? Isn't society itself a warehouse of bad odours?' We would philosophize thus and ignore them.

But a horrid stench that wouldn't go away entered our rooms and began to invade our spaces. At first, no one took it seriously. Usually, a carcass that gave off a powerful stink dried up and shrank in a couple of days, then dwindled to nothing. We expected the stench to vanish soon. But it seemed as if the stench had vowed not to give up until it had made our nostrils feel its fetid strength. We tried to console ourselves with the theory that the stench came from far away, and had carried all the way to our house because of the windy season. No way. The stink was present even when the wind changed direction. It gradually grew in intensity.

In an unprecedented move, all of us joined hands and cleaned the rooms together. The walls shone bright after the cobwebs were removed. The stucco floor acquired a sheen once it was rid of even the small stains. Seeing the skeletons and withered carcasses in the trash, we screwed up our faces and declared that they must have caused the stench. Whenever the cat appeared at any window, we were ready to launch an attack. Frightened by our hostility, the cat kept up a plaintive mewl that circled around the house all through the night. We also took some steps to make the house fragrant. After collecting and throwing out all the trash, we fumigated the rooms with incense. We bought phenyl and sprinkled its solution everywhere. It seemed like the stench was somewhat under control.

The following morning, the stench worsened. Once we were sure that the stench was not coming from the decomposing bodies of small creatures, we wondered what else it could be. Meanwhile, we exchanged gloomy thoughts among ourselves about its impact: that the stink made it difficult to think about anything, that it felt like a worm was burrowing relentlessly through our head, that breathing this foul air would reduce our lifetime by half and that we would become hollow-eyed from prolonged sleep deprivation.

We looked for remedies, like shifting to a different house. After someone mentioned that it could be the sorcery of the seductive ghost – a faceless virgin girl who had hanged herself in that house – we were afraid to stay alone there. With or without offering reasons, some of us began to spend the night out, staying with friends. The stench whirled around relentlessly inside the house, and invaded all the rooms. Although some of us thought that it smelt like fresh, moist shit, no one said it aloud.

In the end, that hunch turned out to be true. A friend who ventured to the back of the house for some reason rushed back in panic. Along with disgust, pride at having discovered something also glowed on his face. It was nothing extraordinary. The pipe from the toilet to the septic tank had broken in the middle. The shit from the toilet had come out through the breach and spread in a heap at the back of the house. Hidden among the overgrown thickets of parthenium shrubs, the shit heap wasn't readily visible. Little by little, the smell had travelled outward, entered the house with a stranger's diffidence and, in time, begun to roam freely inside all the rooms. While each of us had solutions ready at hand for all the world's problems, we didn't know what to do about this one. We could only exchange vacant stares with others around us.

~

That tumbler had neither been preserved in safe custody through many generations of a feudal dynasty nor been blessed with the royal saliva of a king who had ruled his territory with matchless strength. It was just a plain, ordinary tumbler. Here is a note that tries to create a puranic tale about its arrival in our household: For one of our first-day-of-the-month parties, an extra head, over and above the number of steel tumblers in our possession, had turned up. If it were just cold drinks, the bottles themselves could serve as tumblers. But it was a booze party. If someone got more than his share, appeasing the others wouldn't be an easy task. So an extra tumbler became absolutely essential. A tumbler could only be purchased at a shop about four or five kilometres from our deserted locality. There were no street lamps in that area. There were no streets either. Walking through those dense woods at night was never easy. But there was an 'annachi' provision store in our area, just as there was one in every locality. We knew that tumblers were not sold there. Even so, out of some fond hope we decided to ask them. After plucking some plantains from a bunch at the front of the shop, we slipped in our question about a tumbler. 'If you buy a packet of coffee powder or detergent, you get this for free,' said the shopkeeper, showing us a tumbler. We bought it right away.

Among our steel tumblers, it stood out defiantly like a big leaf cup. The brown of its bottom half brought to mind an obese body sitting cross-legged on the floor. Everyone was eager to reach for the tumbler and claim it for themselves. Along with its majestic allure, its capacity was also a reason for our eagerness; in other words, the craving to get a little extra booze. Moreover, given its light weight and ease of handling, you could hold it normally even in a highly inebriated condition.

~

No one was interested in discussing the problem. Silence prevailed for the next couple of days, as if we had already vacated the house. Communist as well as computer brains proposed the same solution: that we should vacate immediately. But if an alternative solution was found, everyone was willing to change his mind – that much space wouldn't be available in any other rented accommodation.

When the man from the neighbouring house – 'neighbouring' meant a furlong away – dropped in to discuss something with us, he saw the gloom and panic writ large on our faces, expressed his condolences and thereby came to learn about our woes. 'Is that all?' he said dismissively, and assured us that it was not an insurmountable problem. Then he began to narrate his own story in elaborate detail, from buying a plot in that distant suburb to bravely constructing and moving into the first house in the area. After establishing that he was the oldest resident of the neighbourhood, he turned finally to the toilet problem. But until then, listening to his story was like having scalding hot water poured on our feet but being unable to cry out. In the course of the conversation, a few of us slipped away, pretending we had work to do.

Finally, our neighbour informed us that the municipality's garbage collection truck visited the area once in a rare while and that two or three sweepers also came along with it. If we gave them ten or twenty rupees, they would clean up the mess, he told us. He also let it be known that the driver of the garbage truck was a long-time acquaintance. We told him that in case we were not home when the truck came by, he could bring the personnel to our house and negotiate the deal on our behalf.

We prayed for the sweepers to arrive soon. When there are so many concocted stories about the coming of the lord, and so many who believe in them and wait eagerly for god to appear, there was nothing wrong in our belief that the sweepers would actually show up. We gathered at the front gate of our house, to escape that stinging whiplash of a stench, and kept throwing brief, expectant glances at the entry road to our locality. Sometimes we imagined hearing the sound of an approaching truck. Though we hadn't quite arranged for garlands and brass plates for aarti, we were mentally prepared for it.

With a heart full of compassion that did not let its devotees' faith go in vain, the truck chose an auspicious Sunday to visit our locality. It entered slowly, shaking and juddering over the humps and trenches on our roads, as if over the earth's natural terrain. By means of our enthusiastic leaps and cries of jubilation, the news travelled fast in all directions. Pulling on a shirt, one of my housemates rushed off to fetch our neighbour. Another positioned himself in the middle of the road to signal the truck to stop. A third went to check if the passage to the backyard of the house was usable. The smell stalked and drove us all to action. Our former enthusiasm was back again.

The sweeper's appearance reminded us of film comedians from a bygone era. His thin and bony physique looked as if it would break into pieces and collapse any minute. He was quite tall, though. He wore nothing on his upper body. To cover the lower part, he had wrapped a length of rough cotton fabric around his waist, like a lungi. When he laughed, baring his betel-stained teeth, we could only feel disgust towards him. But we put on expressions that were meant to deny any such feelings.

The 'senior' – our neighbour – brought him into the house. Standing about fifteen feet away, we pointed in the direction of the area he should inspect. He moved in between the parthenium shrubs as if he was taking a stroll in a garden. He bent down suddenly and pulled out four or five plants which had grown tall and big. The spot widened into a clearing. As soon as we saw the shit spread in a heap like a swarm of ash-coloured fungi grazing the ground, we covered our nostrils.

Paying little heed to anything else, the sweeper roved further and further, like a dog following a scent. After sauntering back and forth through that jungle of brushwood trying to find the leak, he discovered the septic tank.

We were looking at it for the first time ourselves. Half-buried in the ground, it was trapped on all sides by overgrown grass. He walked around it twice. With flaring nostrils, his face looked very serious. His eyes had bulged out and turned red. He made a face and laughed, like a madman. His brain must have sent him a victory signal that the territory belonged to him now. Then he started walking towards us. Unconsciously, all of us took a step back or sideways, as if to escape from an evil creature.

It was impossible to accept the figure as human. None of the men who did such work, as we had conjured up during our discussions, bore any resemblance to him. All of them possessed a minimal degree of human refinement. They didn't roam around like animals, guided solely by their sense of smell. They finished their jobs without delay, effortlessly, as if by a magic spell. We could offer solutions to such people. But this man? Unaware that the stench was gnawing at our intestines, how calmly he stood there and bargained with us!

He explained the cause of the mishap as well as the nature of the job we expected of him. The pipe that led from the toilet to the septic tank was broken. Perhaps the water buffaloes that had come there to graze when the house was lying vacant had stomped on it. Dirt had entered the pipe and blocked the passage. He had to remove the blockage and close the breach with a coat of cement.

The way he opened his mouth like a frog and spoke like a tin box rolling around was obscene. To hear him raise his voice all of a sudden and then lower it instantly to a whimper was terribly annoying. The money he demanded made us even more angry. He wanted five hundred rupees.

The 'senior', after describing his own role as a negotiator to the sweeper, finally told him the amount was too much for the job. 'I have to put my hand in your shit, sir.' Our ears could not bear to listen to him repeat this several times, like a sorcerer's chant. We were so enraged that we wanted to tell him, 'Go away, you dog,' and chase him away. But we had no other option.

The 'senior' came over to us. Leading us to a far corner, he asked us in a conspiratorial whisper, 'How much should we pay him?' As if the sweeper had forgotten what our neighbour had told him, he prowled here and there like a kitten and said firmly and clearly, so we could hear it, 'You call this ground, do you? It's shit, sir, your shit.' We thought it would be a good idea if he or the lot of us moved away from that spot immediately. The look on our faces was driving him to a manic frenzy. Every time he pronounced the word 'shit', he looked pointedly at us, made a face and broke into a grin. Highly satisfied after seeing how nettled and disgusted we were by the word, he repeated it over and over again.

We decided that we would offer three hundred initially and go up to four hundred if necessary. His antics confirmed that he would not take a lesser amount. Our neighbour went over to him again and communicated our offer courteously. He would not yield. 'I have to scoop up the shit, sir. If you know anyone who'll shovel this shit for you, you can call him, sir.' Repeating this many times over, he refused to come down from five hundred. Since our landlord was going to pay the extra hundred anyway, we wanted to say yes to him. But our neighbour stood firm at four hundred. Shouldn't his word carry some weight, after all? Meanwhile, the driver of the garbage truck came over and asked wearily, 'Are you still at it?' On assessing the situation, he told the sweeper, 'Do it, man...is four hundred not enough for you?' 'I'll give you four hundred rupees, sir,' the sweeper said defiantly. 'Let's see you put your hand in this shit.' 'That's enough, man. Just do it,' the driver told him in a peremptory tone, and he agreed reluctantly.

Promising to start the work soon, he asked for an advance of one hundred rupees. 'Give him, sir,' the driver urged us strongly when we vacillated a bit. Once the money was handed over, the man wanted a bicycle for an hour. We had a bicycle which was locked and parked inside the house. As soon as the sweeper made his request, the owner of the bicycle replied before anyone else, 'We don't have a cycle, pa.' We imagined him touching the bicycle, and us touching it after it became filthy with his touch, and felt a deep sense of revulsion. It seemed like his entire body was made of shit and gave off a foul smell all the time. As he walked away, swinging his hands and feet, we saw shit scattering and falling all along his path. His speech too carried a fetid odour. Spraying filth, he walked out majestically from our house.

Only half an hour had passed since the truck's arrival.

~

The tumbler might have felt sad and proud at the same time – the loneliness of being unable to see anyone of its own kind and the grief of lying on the shelf, neglected and covered in dust, for a long time; but at the same time, even if it was only on rare occasions, pride at the way people competed and fought with one another for the pleasure of holding it in their hands, and the arrogance of standing taller than all the other glasses and exerting authority over them. When someone said that he had seen a tumbler exactly like it in a tea stall in his village, another fellow retorted that he was trying to get over the dejection of not getting hold of it that evening by trying to belittle its stature. Still another fellow remarked derisively that village tea stalls only had glass tumblers; so how could a plastic tumbler – such a pretty-looking multicoloured one at that – have ended up there? In this way, the tumbler also became the subject of a minor skirmish along with the main topic of discussion that night.

~

He returned on unsteady feet, carrying a long steel rod and a bag of cement. His laughter now reeked of country liquor. Our facial expressions indicated that none of us could stand the smell. His bulging eyes guided his body forward. He seemed to float gently on a carpet of parthenium flowers. In no time at all, he got to work. Without asking for assistance, he moved the metal cover of the septic tank all by himself. His movements showed that he was highly skilled at his work. He looked like a dog kneeling and smiling.

We stood at a distance and watched him. We thought that if we went closer, we might faint; if we inhaled the shit, we might develop an aversion for food or feel nauseous. Nevertheless, we wanted to see him work and check whether he was doing the job properly. We were afraid that he might cheat us otherwise.

He seemed to pay no attention to anything except his work. He inserted the steel rod inside the pipe that led to the septic tank and pushed it using all his strength. The mud block must have become really hardened. The rod refused to go further in. Suddenly, he jumped into the septic tank. His face became invisible. We could only see the movement of the hair on the back of his head. The brown streaks in his hair glinted in the sunlight. He raised his hands and gripped the rod. Now his task was easy. The force behind pushing the rod in was not wasted. He held the rod and thrust it in with the fervour of attacking and felling an enemy. It seemed as if the pipe itself was about to be uprooted; the ground above shook with the impact. The pounding noise escaped through the hole and was heard feebly outside. I wanted to warn him sternly that he might break the pipe. Many words stood ready at the tip of our tongues. But a fear restrained us. He might be capable of using more terrible words than us. Amid the rustling movement of parthenium shrubs, the passage in the pipe opened up abruptly.

Everyone could breathe peacefully now. We didn't have to inhale the stink any more. We could drive away the ghosts that haunted our rooms. Our high-spirited revelries would resume. There would be no more talk of vacating the house.

He climbed out of the septic tank.

We closed our eyes and turned our faces away. The shit that streamed out when the mud block in the pipe had given way was smeared in lumpy bits all over his face. Even in that condition, he bared his teeth and grinned at us. It was like a pile of shit opening its mouth wide. It gave us the creeps. His thin torso was also coated in shit. He tugged at his hair and began to straighten it. We had ceased all movement and speech. Looking up, he said, 'Shit,' and laughed. That word felt like an angry whiplash on our skin. The relentless lashing echoed through all the rooms, settled and spread out on the ground, filled the sky with its sound, pulled out all the organs of nature as blood gushed out.

'Some water to wash this shit off.' The words calmed us and got us moving. My senses merely watched a fellow run inside and come back with the dirty, moss-covered bucket that was kept in the toilet and an empty can with a hole in it. He kept them at a distance from the man and escaped to safety. Scattering pieces of shit along the way, the man walked to the bucket and washed himself.

But how could he ever become clean again? What could he do about the shit that must have entered through the pores on his skin? How would he rid himself of the reek of shit that had laid siege to him from all sides? It was not slush whose smell could be washed away with a bucket of water, was it? But he washed himself with the water, and removing the cloth wrapped around his waist, wiped himself dry. (Fortunately, a pair of small briefs with several holes in it covered his private parts.) His wiping, only moderately thorough, made it appear as if his aim was only to get rid of the water off his body, not the shit. Again he looked like a funny, strange beast to us. 'Water,' he said once more. Which of us dared to go near him, touch and lift the bucket, and bring it back? But he said clearly again, 'I want some water to drink.' Again, all of us were gripped by a feeling of dismay. One fellow who felt brave enough to handle the situation stepped forward.

'Bring it in a sombu,' the man ordered. 'We don't have a sombu,' the one who had volunteered replied. 'Bring it in the utensil you drink from,' the man said.

When the volunteer came back, he had the plastic tumbler in his hand. Though we had so many steel tumblers in the house, he had picked the plastic one. We, who had regularly fought for that plastic tumbler, didn't say a word in its support now; instead, we praised the fellow who had chosen it for the sweeper. He was about to keep the brimming tumbler on the ground. 'Give it to me, sir,' the sweeper said. None had the courage to do it. Chortling triumphantly, the sweeper raised the tumbler to his mouth and drank from it with his snout, like a pig. It was perhaps his intention to drench the tumbler in shit. 'Here, sir,' the man held it out. 'Keep it over there,' someone said. The sweeper himself chose a spot in the corner, next to the wall.

The tumbler appeared to move and tremble in the breeze. But no one rushed or jostled with the others to pick it up and hold it close to his chest. We thought it was a suitable spot for the tumbler. Only then did we realize that there was nothing special about it. It was old and worn. On a closer look, we found that its wide bottom, brown in colour, was a sirattai, the bald shell of a half coconut; its finely wrought upper half was glass.

Translated from 'Pee'

9

Sanctuary

Visiting my native village during the summer vacation was not as much fun as it used to be. My enthusiasm subsided in a matter of days and I felt like I was stranded on a desert island. After a late morning in bed, followed by some chores, breakfast and a stroll, next on the day's agenda were the tea stall and the newspaper. Then it was time for lunch and a nap. The evening and early hours of the night were the worst of all.

My childhood friends, who still lived in the village, had morphed into either married dolts expected to be home by six or small-time businessmen who shouted, 'See you around!' as they whizzed past on their two-wheelers, just as they would perfunctorily raise their hands to piously pat their own cheeks while passing a temple. The old men, for their part, drove me away with their inane questions: 'You are still studying, aren't you?' Why was I on vacation? Who asked for this, exactly? I couldn't help feeling frustrated and annoyed.

My only consolation was a visit to the public well for a few hours in the afternoon to escape the scorching summer heat. The well was crowded with boys of various ages gambolling in the water. Some were learning to swim by clinging to a water-gourd shell, while practised swimmers jumped into the water, laughing at the learners. Unable to mingle with the boys, I stood in a corner. Sometimes I dived in, swam a lap around the well and came back to stand in the same spot. Watching their antics brought my childhood memories bubbling up to the surface.

But what could I do? I was like a patient lying in a corner, in no shape to partake in the joyous celebration of a festival. Though I could get up on the mound, jump into the well, dive all the way to the bottom and play around in the water, none of the boys took the slightest notice of me. I was not even a small insect in their eyes. Some of their parents might have attended primary school with me. Anyway, for how long could I derive pleasure from merely watching others play? Even if I stood in waist-deep water, my upper body burned in the heat, and I would discreetly climb out of the well and slip away. In any case, who took notice of my coming and going?

Someone who doesn't know how to swim can only sit by the steps, scoop up the water and pour it over himself again and again. I did the same thing, but where the well was a little deeper. Nothing stays the same forever, though. Over time, at least a minor change is bound to occur, isn't it? As if giving me a chance to reveal myself and make an impression on them, one of the small boys ran towards me and hugged my legs.

'Look at him, anna. He keeps holding me down in the water, just like that.'

It was a cry for succour. Responsibility for providing him immediate refuge had landed on my head.

'Why do you do this, da?' I asked the perpetrator in a threatening tone. It seemed to fall on deaf ears.

'Dei, you scared little punk! Come out if you have the guts!' The bully challenged the boy hiding behind me, and dived flamboyantly into the water. I couldn't tolerate such behaviour. Was my voice so lowly and contemptible? How arrogant of the little tyke! I leapt after him, caught him by the hair and dunked his head in the water. When he came up for air, I pushed him down again.

'Anna...let me go, 'na...let me go, 'na...' I didn't release him till he was reduced to stammering and pleading. In that moment, the well seemed to become aware of my existence and sent ripples across the water. From then on, power over the well passed entirely into my hands.

My regular tasks included scolding the little monkeys who, instead of climbing up the steps, tried to clamber up the roots of trees and protecting those who didn't know swimming, as well as giving them a helping hand to climb out of the well.

'Look at him, anna! He is shoving me.'

'Tell him not to push me down, anna.'

'Ask him to give my shorts back, anna.'

I became the overlord who received their

complaints, enquired into them and meted out due punishment. My age and physical strength had transformed me into a petty monarch of that round well. Only on rare occasions was I ruthless in exercising my authority. Even then, it was only meant to frighten the boys. At other times, I was so gentle in using my power that the boys were hardly aware that I was ordering them about. If I sensed that I was about to be disobeyed, I announced the breach as a concession. The days passed smoothly. Besides, I was happy at having created a kingdom for myself. I became a frog that lay in the water for at least four or five hours daily.

When I was little, there used to be a minimum of two or three groups among the boys. The older boys would jump in separately and play their own games. Boys of that age group rarely came to the well now. They must have turned into wind-up toys employed in the bazaars of the city. Those at the well were not yet trapped in the daily routine of wearing a tie and boarding a bus to school. They were free birds studying in – no, just attending – the primary school run by the government. I feared that they might see me as a schoolmaster strutting around with a cane in his hand. I was also fed up with being the sole authority in a territory where I faced no competition. Soon, I was ready to give up my position. I didn't know fully yet what I was after. My primary motive must have been to win back my childhood.

I announced my stepping down through a proposal: 'I also want to play a round of catch with you.'

None of them was willing to accept this gesture. They must have feared that I would infiltrate their circle, break it up and destroy it forever. As we kept staring at each other's faces, there was no sound except for a big chunk of mud sliding from a corner of the well into the water. I asked them again in an almost pleading tone. They wouldn't trust me so quickly. They thought I would use my authority to insist on my inclusion, but were disappointed. Without getting in their way, I swam by myself in a different part of the well for some time, then went home. The next day, I changed my wish to a request. My tone came down to the level of begging.

'Please let me join the game, da.'

It must have given them joy and hope. They agreed immediately. There was a condition, though. Four of them would team up and try to tap me. However, I had to tap all four players for a 'strike'. By the normal rules of the game, it amounted to cheating. But perhaps my adult's physique made them impose this condition.

They discovered my prowess underwater in no time. Unable to cope with being chased by four players, I lost before I had gone halfway around the well. And unsuccessful in my attempts to tap all four players, I kept swimming all over the place for a long time. Being little boys gave them plenty of advantages. Like tadpoles, they jumped into the water and disappeared with great ease.

It took me a long time to twist my body like an ageing snake and start moving. I wasn't adept at swimming in deep water either. There were a couple of boys who were capable of diving all the way to the floor and coming back up. Even those who swam clumsily on the surface kept lifting their behinds rhythmically to gather speed. I became tired very quickly and needed to stop every now and then to catch my breath before I could resume. That I could not best them in any manner must have boosted their morale.

It pleased me not a little to recognize that I too was like them, save for my physical development. I was gradually travelling backward by ten–fifteen years. With my hands clutching the aerial roots of time, I leapt across the years. My mind began to roam freely, bereft of any worries about the present or the future. I wandered as I pleased, ignoring or evading the rebukes from my mother that I was wallowing in the water all the time. I was keen on bringing within my grasp the realm of freedom that lay trapped inside the circular expanse of that well. The boys came by my house to invite me to the well. I too went to their homes to invite them. There remained no difference between us.

In the game of catch too, I came to be treated like one of them. I wasn't given any special concession. I wasn't a stranger in their world any more. After dividing ourselves into two teams, we held hands in a circle and picked the chaser through a preliminary counting-out game. While the chaser stood on one side, players from the rival team moved to the opposite side. Each of us had to swim past the chaser without getting caught and tap the uddi, our counterpart from the opposing team, standing behind the chaser. No matter how long we played, we never grew tired of this game.

'Dei! Come on, let's toss and find out who wins,' I would shout at the player who would falsely claim that he had tapped me.

In response, he would catch me by my hair and lift me up, and I would struggle and fight with him. If, in the heat of battle, my hand or leg brushed against him, I countered his triumphant shouts with: 'Where did you tap me? It was I who tapped you!' I would jump into the well from the mound outside with a war cry: 'Daaa...aai!' Gradually, the rigidities in my body disappeared. I was going back in time even physically. My hands and feet began to shrink. Those legs, as ugly and broad as shovels, and arms, as wide as winnowing pans, became elegant. The hairs in my moustache and beard fell away. My face became clear and guileless like a field bund shorn of all grass. I could dive underwater and swim with the natural ease of a fingerling.

All worldly matters that had tormented me fled my mind. My body became so light that I was able to climb up a tree root that had snaked inside the well and jump back into the water from the top. My young friends were pleased at my agility.

They were happy for the addition of one more person to their group. Even if I spent many hours daily jumping into the well, the water never entered and blocked my ears nor did my head feel heavy. In one straight dive, I could go all the way down to the floor and bring back a handful of mud. The changes wrought in me frightened and worried my mother. 'Why has he become like this?' she started complaining to everyone. She must have feared that she might have to bring me up all over again. She unloaded a torrent of abuse on the boys who came to fetch me and chased them away. It wasn't too hard to give her the slip and run away to the well.

I wanted to tell her:

'Amma...you don't have to bring me up one more time. I will stay like this forever. My friends will grow up and leave the well, but I'll stay the same. I'll be here, felicitating those who go away and welcoming the new arrivals, the same as ever.'

But there was a thorn of worldliness that was still stuck in my mind. Beyond the reach of my sharp fingernails and eluding the scope of my vision, it was stuck somewhere in me, one with my flesh. I was still holding on to something. The real world had not entirely let go of me. Which angler's line was still tugging at me, I wondered. Though I tried to pull it out and throw it away, I couldn't find the free end of the knot.

Something happened one day to rid me of the weary expression on my lustreless face. One of my friends wanted to catch a few of the tiny fish that were nibbling at our ankles and breed them in the fish tank at his home. All of us joined in. We thought it would be easy if we stretched our hands wide and caught the fish as they came close to the surface to breathe. However, the fish would instinctively sense even the slightest disturbance from the depths below and move away. We tried our best in all parts of the well, but we couldn't catch any fish. Suddenly a boy said:

'If we have a piece of cloth, we can use it to catch the fish.'

Not one had a stitch on him. Everyone turned towards me at the same time.

'Dei, take off your loincloth and give it to us,' a boy shouted without any qualms.

I hesitated, but only for a moment. I could figure out the knot this time. I pulled the cloth free and threw it at him.

The ripples rise and fall. Rubbing their arms, the fish are laughing among themselves. A baby's tender arms are swinging through the water, which glints with the touch of sunlight. I am gliding smoothly towards the depths...going deeper...and deeper still...

Translated from 'Pugalidam'

10

The Man Who Could Not Sleep

Sleep had eluded Muthu Pattar for a whole month now. Since he roamed around in the fields and groves all day, he was normally eager to turn in early. Once he lay down, he would fall asleep instantly, as if by magic. No matter how loudly the cattle bellowed and the dogs barked, the old woman still had to wake him up. 'Sleeps like a wretched corpse. There's so much noise around, but it doesn't affect him,' she would grumble. From his childhood days, sleep was always a big asset for him. They would never send him to guard the cattle pen or the threshing floor because he might fall asleep. 'Even a drunk wakes up at midnight, but this boy will open his eyes only after sunrise,' they said. And he never ran short of that sleep. 'The man doesn't mull over things in his mind and confuse himself. That's why he gets such blissful sleep,' men of his vintage would remark enviously.

He didn't know where that glorious sleep had vanished. Lying with his six-foot frame scrunched up in a rope cot that sagged in the middle no matter how many times the ropes were fastened, he looked like a small baby fast asleep in the cradle. He would lie in the same position, neither tossing about nor rolling over in his sleep. If he heard someone whining about not being able to sleep, he would say with genuine surprise: 'Is that even possible?' Slothful idlers who lolled around at home all day might lose their sleep, but how could it happen to a man who wandered around with bulls and calves without a moment to stand still? 'Walk in the fields and groves to exercise your legs and have a look around. You'll get sound sleep,' he told them.

Even those men who toiled hard all day complained that they couldn't sleep. 'Ada, when we enter our homes, do we step in wearing our sandals? We go in only after taking them off, right? It works the same way. Before lying down, you should unload all your worries,' he'd say casually. 'How can we unload them? Our worries will leave us only when we die.' He would look at such people with derision. But now, that conviction had been belied by circumstance.

The first night he spent tossing around, unable to sleep, he thought it was a stomach problem. Whenever he ate something that didn't suit him, he suffered from chest pain and a throbbing ache in the legs for a few days. Even then, if he lay down on the cot and rolled over a couple of times, sleep would come to inhabit his eyes. But he couldn't sleep a wink that night. Even when he lay on the cot for a long time with his eyes closed, nothing seemed to happen. Because his eyes were red like a scarlet gourd in the morning, people asked him if he was all right. He didn't know what to say. How could he ever have trouble getting sleep? Feeling somewhat lethargic that evening, he hadn't prepared hot water for his bath; he had bathed with cold water instead. He guessed that could be the reason for his sleeplessness. The body demanded so many of these comforts.

The next day, just before going to sleep, he poured steaming hot water on his body. Even in scorching summer, he was particular about bathing in hot water. 'Roasted by summer heat your body is like a ripe fruit, and you pour boiling hot water on it? Are you at all human?' the old woman would scold him. 'Only a buffalo knows the joys of wallowing in mud,' he'd say with a mocking laugh. 'If this buffalo wasn't around, how would you have survived?' the old woman would hit back. A hot water bath would always bring on sleep. A drowsy feeling set in as soon as one wiped the body dry. And in that state, if one quickly swallowed a couple of morsels of rice, one could lie down immediately and go to sleep. But on that day, the body burned like a blaze and sleep proved elusive.

His rope cot lay in the eastern corner of the thatched shed. Rain or sunshine, he always slept in the eastern corner. When he was a little child, his mother used to keep her cot there and sleep on it, hugging him to her side. Sleeping there made him feel as safe as he had felt in his mother's arms. But he never told anyone about it. He avoided staying overnight outside the village. On the couple of occasions when he was forced to spend the night elsewhere, he never slept a wink. But how could a spot where he had slept since he was a baby become alien to him? He thought of changing the spot, just in case. If you lie down where an evil spirit has come to stay, you won't be able to sleep. But the new spot he chose was also inhabited by an evil spirit, it seemed. His eyes just wouldn't close. He concluded that the fault must lie somewhere else.

Someone had put an evil spell on him, perhaps? Was he leading such a grand life, in a palace with a host of servants, that someone had reason to put a spell on him? The only likely person was his wife, the woman who had lived with him for the past forty years. Having borne the atrocities of his robust youth, she wouldn't do such a thing at the fag end of his life. What did she know, anyway, apart from the dung on the cattle shed floor and smoke from the wood stove? His sons lived separately, each in his own thatched shed. He caused them no trouble. Once they sprouted wings, he had sent his young ones out to seek their own food. Keeping a piece of land for himself, he had divided the rest among them. Fortunately, he had only two sons and no daughter. If Pattar passed away, there was going to be no shower of gold through the roof for anyone. All that would remain were four or five tattered loincloths. If close relatives were ruled out, where would a sorcerer spring from, food bundle in hand, to cast a spell?

His intake of four balls of millet rice at every meal had reduced to two. 'From the beginning, cooking for him was endless toil. I am glad it's come down now.' The old woman was pleased. Pattar's work had also become tardy. He never used to sleep during the day. If he stretched out now during the day, his eyes laughed at him as if to say: we don't close even when it's pitch-dark, so how can you keep us shut on this blistering hot, arid afternoon? He tried using sacred ash enriched with curative mantras, wearing an amulet on his arm and arranging sessions of ritual chanting. During chanting, Songa Pattar mocked him, 'What's up, Muthu? You are not getting any sleep, is it? If you tell anyone, they're going to laugh at you.' It was only after much pleading from Muthu that he was persuaded to believe it himself and do the chanting. 'The sleep demon which had possessed you when you were little has left you only now,' he teased Muthu. But the sleep that had got away seemed to stay away permanently. If the wife walked away in a huff, she would go to her mother's house; the husband could go there after a few days, beg and cajole her, and bring her back. How was he to find out where his sleep had fled?

The old man treated a lot of ailments in cattle and humans. Back in the day, he had sat in the local pyol school for a few years. Thus, he was used to reading – slowly, putting the letters together for each syllable – medical treatises as well as a compilation of treatments, inscribed on palm leaves. If a patient came to him for treatment, he would sit down immediately with a bundle of palm leaves. Although he knew very well what the problem was and the treatment he should prescribe, he would pretend to look them up in the palm leaves. Only then would the patient be satisfied. Couldn't such a learned man diagnose his own ailment? What was the use of treating people for so many years?

Sleeplessness as a distinct ailment was not to be found in the palm leaves. It was invariably associated with some other complaint. He could not identify this other complaint of his. Everything seemed perfectly normal. Jettisoning the idea that some outsider must have robbed him of sleep, he started thinking about his problem. While he was walking or sitting under the tree after leading the goats to pasture – which is to say, nearly all the time – he thought obsessively about his own ailment. But even after thinking for a long time, he couldn't find anything.

He was coming back from the fields on a blazing hot afternoon. As usual, he was immersed in thought. There was a bundle of grass on his head. He always preferred to go in the afternoon for harvesting grass. There would be nary a crow in the fields. He could pull out as much grass as he liked from anyone's field. In Kathan's land, which was covered over by a wild growth of small creepers, he had pilfered grass from nearly half a section of the field. It was a big bundle. If anyone asked him, he would say derisively, 'When there's all the grass I need in my own land, why would I enter some idiot's field?' Insects crawled over his face and body. It was nothing unusual for insects in the grass to crawl on the upper body. But now they crawled on his thoughts too. When the itching became too much for him, he abruptly threw the bundle on the ground.

'Why, thatha! Was it too heavy?' The fellow asking him the question was Murugesan, a young lad whom Muthu had known since he was a newborn. Murugesan must be slightly older than his grandson. He took care of his family's farming activities as well as held a job at the spinning mill. The spinning mill was five or six miles from their village. In the mill, Gounder boys were given preference in recruitment. For small farmers surviving on a bit of land and a few heads of cattle, a job at the spinning mill meant additional income. Even if the salary was less than expected, they would quietly do their work. People of other castes couldn't be trusted; they would start holding up flags and shouting slogans at the slightest provocation. Murugesan got a job under that scheme. He did his job diligently and honestly. Didn't his farming work suffer, then? His mother managed everything by herself.

Murugesan wouldn't stay back at home even for a day. If he was asked to take leave to attend a marriage or some other function, he'd get angry. He went on leave only when the mill management took pity on him and gave him a day off. Similarly, he would never spend even a paisa from his salary. He would commute the five miles to the spinning mill every day on his bicycle. He had a special way with that bicycle. He spent half an hour with it every morning, cleaning it thoroughly and making sure that everything was all right before taking it out. He would bring home even the karupatti – palm jaggery – given by the spinning mill and sell it to some villager. At the mill, tiny cotton particles mixed in the air could enter the lungs and stick there, causing tuberculosis. Karupatti was given to the workers as a preventive. At least one block of karupatti had to be eaten in a week to keep the throat and windpipe cleansed. If this was pointed out to him, he would reply casually: 'I'll handle it when it comes.' There were people willing to pay three rupees for a big slab of karupatti. He was very shrewd that way.

All his parents had was a hut with a leaky roof and a mud wall that dissolved and collapsed when it rained. They couldn't afford to buy enough palm fronds to thatch the roof properly. Only when the situation became so bad that they couldn't live there any more did they scrounge loans from sundry sources and finally thatch the roof. It happened once in ten years, like a temple festival. They couldn't even afford maintenance repairs to that roof every year. But as an adult now, Murugesan was building a house with brick walls. He was going to use block tiles on the roof, they said. Who used handmade tiles nowadays? It was block tiles everywhere. The work was easy too. You only had to know how to fix tiles on the reeper wood. If a tile broke, anyone could remove it and replace it with another. Marriage only after completing the house, Murugesan had told his family. As if his wife would conceive only in a house with a tiled roof. The owner of a tiled-roof house will get a bride from a wealthy family – that must have been the reason behind Murugesan's stance.

Muthu Pattar was very eager to talk to Murugesan. Whatever his private thoughts about Murugesan, he would always say a few flattering words to the young man. In response, Murugesan would also treat him with affection. He often took the liberty of asking the old man for suggestions. When he started constructing the house, he had asked, 'Will it be enough if the roof is at twice a man's height?' 'Ada, you're such a buffoon. How will it be enough? If you stand upright and stretch your hand, it will strike the roof. Don't think about the expense. Keep the roof at a height of twenty feet. Let the air circulate freely inside.' Murugesan liked the old man's suggestion. A pity I don't have a son like him who'll listen to my advice, thought Muthu. His sons were bent on contradicting or doing the opposite of whatever he told them. They showed him no respect at all.

'So, how is the work on the house progressing?' he enquired of Murugesan. In fact, he had been closely measuring the progress of the house whenever he passed that way. He knew it even better than Murugesan. Even so, he *had* to begin the conversation this way, didn't he?

Murugesan complained at great length: construction work hadn't progressed as expected, the workers didn't come regularly, and even when they did, they cheated by not doing any work but received their wages without any cuts. The same words of complaint that his boss at the spinning mill spouted every week at the time of disbursing wages issued now from Murugesan's mouth. Finally, he concluded:

'It's such hard work to build a small house with a tiled roof. We can only imagine the trouble that people who put up those big palaces must go through.'

Muthu Pattar said a few consoling words to

Murugesan.

'You're an adult now, Murugesan. And you're building a house. Keep well, young man.'

He lifted the grass bundle with Murugesan's help, placed it on his head and started walking. Insects continued to crawl on his face and upper body. His shed was just a hundred feet away. Before he reached there, an idea passed through his mind. Even after toiling in the fields for fifty–sixty years, the only constant in his life was this thatched shed. Even that shed dated back to his father's time. He couldn't even afford to thatch the roof once in three or four years. He tried to cope with the rainy season by inserting an extra frond of palm on the leaky side of the roof and covering the roof with jute cloth. Even then, raindrops would pierce the roof and descend into the house like a string of fine needles. 'It's my fate to spend all my days in this shed. Not for nothing do they say, "You can live in a weeping house, but not in a leaking one." But what's the use? This was destined to be my lot,' the old woman would hint obliquely. Seeing no other way out, he would cadge loans from here and there and thatch the roof.

But this boy Murugesan was so young: as they

said, he hadn't even sprouted three leaves yet. He was already building a house with a tiled roof. He spoke about the toil of those who built palaces. It must mean that a plan for building a palace was already incubating in his mind. Oh, he might even do it. For someone who built a tiled-roof house at twenty-five, would it be such a great feat to build a palace at fifty? After throwing down the bundle of grass, he cleared his throat and spat angrily. He felt as if his whole face was smeared with that ball of spittle. He cast a glance towards Murugesan's house. It was a small house with two rooms. The brick walls had been raised to a man's height.

'When you are old, you should do the work you still can, come home and lie down quietly. Why do you have to think so much? Are you going to capture a fortress at the fag end of your life? What's your problem, then? You have filled your belly with food, haven't you? Then, why are you slithering around like a hungry snake?' The old lady spoke a lot. Her jabbering fell on Pattar's ears merely as a series of incoherent sounds. Even if she wasn't there, her voice would keep reverberating all over that thatched shed. He knew what it would say at any given moment. He would make sense of it by combining it with the noise of house lizards. The wood stove was in the eastern corner of the shed. The noise of lizards came frequently from that corner. He would decipher its meaning by considering where it was coming from and at which moment. That voice was his only consolation.

Night or day, whenever his eyes turned towards Murugesan's house, he'd unconsciously look up. Workers would appear every now and then. He'd engage them in conversation. 'Poor boy. He is saving every last paisa to build this house. Don't betray him,' he told them. 'If we do, will that money stay with us, thatha? Are we going to build a palace and rule for a thousand years? Whether we are alive or not, our work will stay neat and honest,' the supervisor would reply. The wall was coming up on all four sides. When he went to work in the fields and came back, the wall would have risen by half a yard in that one session. It would seem like a miracle to Muthu. In an empty space with nothing in it, the wall was coming up quickly like an anthill. Murugesan lived within the village. But if he built the house here, surrounded by agricultural land, he could make it more spacious. He had chosen this site because it was also convenient for tending goats and cattle. 'It's on the strength of having you as my neighbour that I am building a house and moving here,' he said. 'I am happy to hear that. Come here by all means. What are we going to carry with us when we die? We are only here to help one another,' was Muthu's generous response. Whenever he saw his sons, he felt angry and agitated, and he abused them freely.

'Look at Murugesan. He is the ideal son. What are you guys good for? Your father's life was spent in a thatched shed. Did you ever think of raising money and building a tiled-roof house? Bloody, incompetent dogs.'

His sons were confused. They couldn't understand what had suddenly happened to the old man. He had never talked in this manner. 'Get on in life without giving cause for people to talk ill of you,' was the advice he'd given them often.

'Indeed. You have earned bundles of money and stacked them in the grain vat. We'll keep drawing from it to build a house, right? Do you want us to build a house on borrowed money and repay by selling what we have now? We just want to keep what we have. Go on!' the sons retaliated for their part. Not even one said, even for form's sake, 'Yes, I'll build a house.'

Once Muthu got back after speaking to Murugesan, myriad thoughts raced through his mind. He was restive. Normally, a couple of words with Murugesan would make him feel like he had got back something which was lost; it was the strength of his youthful vitality, thought Muthu. But on that day, in spite of the words spoken and consolation offered, his heart wasn't appeased. Now his sleep was gone. Was it going to be like this from now on? If he took ill from not sleeping at all, he could die soon. He closed his eyes and tried to think of Kariakali, his clan deity. To Kariakali – who appeared inside his eyelids as a picture of fury the moment he thought of her – he would slowly articulate his demands, one by one. But on that night, he could not conjure up Kariakali's face before his eyes no matter how hard he tried. After that failure, careful that he must not wake the old woman, he tiptoed to the entrance. He tightened his loincloth and stretched his arms wide in an attempt to shake off his sluggishness. Then he let out a yawn big enough to tear his mouth. 'Am I ever short of yawns?' he thought wearily to himself and turned inadvertently towards Murugesan's house.

The house looked vivid in the moonlight. It seemed as if someone was welcoming him with both palms joined together. Has the gable wall risen that high, he wondered. The only tasks that remained were cementing and plastering. What would it be like to go near the house, stark in the moonlight, and touch it? All was quiet at midnight. Something propelled him forward. Walking slowly, he went and stood in front of the house. He looked around once. He entered the space enclosed by the walls. Because there was no roof, moonlight shone brightly inside the house too. He touched and caressed the walls. He felt the pleasure of hugging a child to his chest. He rubbed his cheek against the wall. A pleasantly cold feeling spread throughout his body. He stayed like that for a very long time. A hen crowed somewhere.

He came to the wall they had built after erecting the scaffolding earlier that day. With great difficulty, he climbed on to the scaffolding. He made a fist and punched the gable wall they had finished that evening. With the punch, some bricks came loose and dropped down. The few teeth that were still left in his mouth gnashed together. He punched hard again. In spite of his calloused fingers and knuckles, he felt the pain. With the second punch, a cascade of bricks came thudding down.

He climbed down on trembling legs and came out of the house. The sight of the broken wall consoled his heart. Before he reached his shed, he turned around several times and stared at the gable wall. It felt as though a big burden had lifted from him. Once he lay down to sleep, he didn't get up till it was long after sunrise. He was in deep slumber. 'The old man is finally cured of his madness today,' his old wife said to herself.

Translated from 'Kombai Chuvar'

Translator's Note

As a man of Tamil letters, Perumal Murugan is too prolific for anyone to keep up with. He writes engagingly in several genres: novels, short stories, poetry, personal memoirs, and essays in textual criticism, literary history, folklore and so on. Even as a fiction writer, he is far better known for his novels – four are available in English translation, with several more in the offing – than his short stories. Although, over the years, I had read a fair number of his stories as and when they appeared in literary magazines and journals, my in-depth engagement with his short fiction began only after I was commissioned to translate a selection of his stories for the present collection.

Translator's Note

Any reader of Perumal Murugan's novels would have noticed the particular ways in which he uses the form. The author follows an individual's life journey through a certain phase, in her immediate human context – of family, village and region – as well as in the larger social and historical contexts. The reader would also know that social relations – including but not limited to the shifting relationships between various communities – form an important part of his novels, as do local histories and landscapes. The problems of livelihood and survival, too, are integral to the construction of Murugan's novels, which are peopled predominantly by the subaltern communities and individuals of the Kongu region in western Tamil Nadu.

As a translator, I found that Perumal Murugan's short stories offer a very different experience from the novels. The straitened, but potentially magical, space of the short story is used to explore the condition of those who are, most profoundly, on their own in this world. The central character in each story is utterly alone, but not always lonely. How do they end up being so alone? Some are forsaken by others. Some are led there by the treachery of their own delusions. Not a few are trapped in that condition by the slow, inexorable turning of a heedless world. Even when they are alone, they cannot avoid being enmeshed in society, in big and small ways. What happens to them in that precarious situation forms the narrative thread in each story.

Most of the characters inhabit a rural landscape; even the city dwellers among them are villagers afflicted by an acute sense of displacement. Hostage to a jumble of hopes and fears, but only moderate in their yearnings, these ordinary men and women try to cope with the dangers they face as best they can. To be alone is to be vulnerable by default, to lack allies. So most of them go down fighting, and in Murugan's telling, with the fragile dignity of the wounded. It's as if by writing their stories the author is restoring them, in all their humanity, back to this world, our world.

The writer Ashokamitran once told me that a translator must know not only the language but also the story. My engagement with these stories, both as a reader and as a translator, has been a rewarding experience. I hope the reader in English, too, will be moved by these brave and unsung characters, and in the spirit of all things literary, take them to heart.

I am grateful to Perumal Murugan for his confidence in my abilities and for being unfailingly supportive in my interactions with him.

I wish to thank R. Sivapriya and Janani Ganesan, my editors at Juggernaut Books, for their hard work and contribution towards ensuring the quality of the translation. Needless to add, the errors that remain are mine.

16 September 2017 **N. Kalyan Raman**
Chennai

A Note on the Author and Translator

A master storyteller, Perumal Murugan has written award-winning novels, short stories and poems. He is also a professor of Tamil language and literature, and a beloved teacher. His best-known work is the novel *Maadorubagan* (*One Part Woman*) that attracted fierce controversy along with immense acclaim.

N. Kalyan Raman has translated some of the finest and most exciting Tamil writers ranging from Ashokamitran and Devibharathi to Poomani and Perumal Murugan.

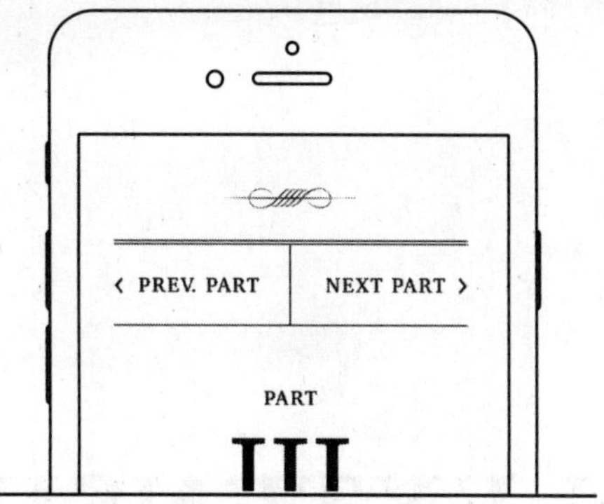

Beautiful Typography

The quality of print transferred to your mobile. Forget ugly PDFs.

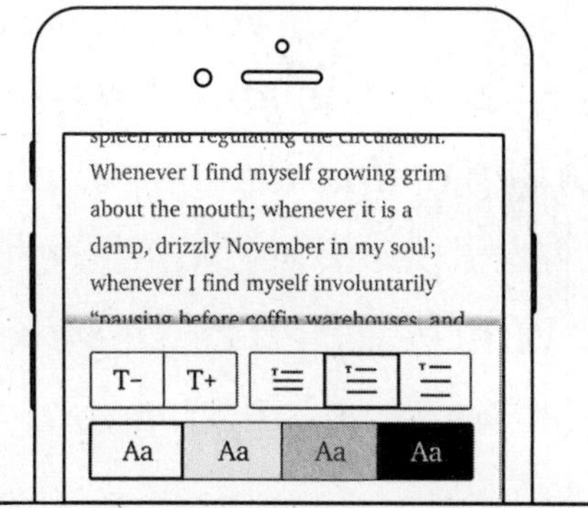

Customizable Reading

Read in the font size, spacing and background of your liking.

AN EXTENSIVE LIBRARY

Including fresh, new, original Juggernaut books from the likes of Sunny Leone, Praveen Swami, Husain Haqqani, Umera Ahmed, Rujuta Diwekar and lots more. Plus, books from partner publishers and loads of free classics. Whichever genre you like, there's a book waiting for you.

juggernaut.in

DON'T JUST READ; INTERACT

We're changing the reading experience from passive to active.

Ask authors questions

Get all your answers from the horse's mouth. Juggernaut authors actually reply to every question they can.

Rate and review

Let everyone know of your favourite reads or critique the finer points of a book – you will be heard in a community of like-minded readers.

Gift books to friends

For a book-lover, there's no nicer gift than a book personally picked. You can even do it anonymously if you like.

Enjoy new book formats

Discover serials released in parts over time, picture books including comics, and story-bundles at discounted rates. And coming soon, audiobooks.

juggernaut.in